MISS CHEYENNE MITCHELL

ETUDE

LitPrime Solutions
East Brunswick Office Evolution
1 Tower Center Boulevard, Ste 1510
East Brunswick, NJ 08816
www.litprime.com
Phone: 1-800-981-9893

© 2024 Miss Cheyenne Mitchell. All rights reserved.

No part of this book may be reproduced, stored in a retrieval system, or transmitted by any means without the written permission of the author.

Published by LitPrime Solutions: 12/19/2024

ISBN: 979-8-88703-442-3(sc)
ISBN: 979-8-88703-443-0(e)

Library of Congress Control Number: 2024922104

Any people depicted in stock imagery provided by iStock are models, and such images are being used for illustrative purposes only.

Certain stock imagery © iStock.

Because of the dynamic nature of the Internet, any web addresses or links contained in this book may have changed since publication and may no longer be valid. The views expressed in this work are solely those of the author and do not necessarily reflect the views of the publisher, and the publisher hereby disclaims any responsibility for them.

"Zobie Moran is growing up in a family that is coping
with poverty, despair and secrecy. Unknown to her
she has a deep connection and shares a terrifying tragedy
with a celebrated female singer. Years pass before the
two women actually meet face to face and form a close, loving
bond with one another. However, fate deals yet another
shocking and unforeseen horror that changes
both of their destinies forever. "

Dedicated To The Lord God Almighty
Who Is The Giver of Creativity and Imagination! Glory!
February, 2009

Contents

Chapter One 1

Chapter Two 8

Chapter Three 12

Chapter Four 18

Chapter Five 26

Chapter Six 28

Chapter Seven 31

Chapter Eight 37

Chapter Nine 40

Chapter Ten 47

Chapter Eleven 53

Chapter Twelve 63

Chapter Thirteen 69

Chapter Fourteen 77

Chapter Fifteen 85

Chapter Sixteen 90

Chapter Seventeen 97

Chapter Eighteen 106

Chapter Nineteen 114

Chapter Twenty 122

Chapter Twenty One 129

Chapter Twenty Two 135

Chapter Twenty Three 139

Chapter One

My name is Zobie which is pronounced Zo-by-a. I am the youngest child of my parents. Everyone in the family calls me 'Zo' for short. I have six brothers and two sisters and we are all two years apart in age. My father has other children besides us. I remain the youngest of all of us so I've heard. He would flash a big, loving smile at me and say, "You're my baby girl, Zo." Need I say more?

My family and I lived in a small town called Harly. My parents, Joseph and Anna Marie Moran, barely made ends meet trying to take care of themselves and nine children. The financial situation in our family was no secret to anybody who knew us. There was hardly enough money for anything except the bills. My father was a Welder at the steel plant in our town. My mother was a home-maker. Her name was, Anna Mae, and she came from a large family herself. She was also the only girl.

Since she was one of the older children in the family my mother had to quit school and go to work in order to bring some money into their household. She was fifteen years old when she began working by cleaning the houses of rich people. It was called 'Day's Work'. When she started it paid twenty dollars a day and she worked no more than six hours each day. The only day she had off was Sunday. Now doing the same thing she earned one hundred and fifty dollars a day, and worked only two or three days a week if she was needed. My maternal grandmother got her the job. It was the only kind of work both of them ever did.

The oldest of my siblings between my parents were my fraternal twin brothers, Zuroi and

Aziel. Under them were my brothers, Angel, Devon and Lee then my two sisters, Venna and Gina. My brother, Damiz, was next to me in age. Obviously, my mother was partial to the letter 'z'. I always believed it was because my grandmother and her were so close and her name was, Zela. That was just my own opinion.

My mother was seventeen years old when my parents first met. According to my Dad, Anna Marie Dackre was a shapely, tall, dark-haired, dark-eyed beauty that he couldn't resist. He was twenty nine years old. So I guess the phrase 'dirty, old man' didn't mean much to him. It also didn't seem to matter to him that he had a wife and four children at home either.

My maternal grandparents wanted to hurt my father in the worst way, especially my grandfather, Berry. My mother has two older brothers, Zane and Whil, who offered to beat my Dad up numerous times. However, my grandparents figured if they did that my mother would've been more driven into my father's arms. So they wouldn't allow my uncles to hurt him although their offer was quite enticing.

My father ran around with my mother for years behind his wife's back. And when Anna Marie turned up pregnant all hell broke loose. My father's wife's name was, Bedelia, and she was twenty five years old when it all started. She caught my parents together one night in a neighborhood bar called 'No Way Out'. The name of the place was named appropriately. It was a wild place and somebody was always getting hurt there. A few people even got killed in there before it was finally shut down.

From all that I heard it was the first and only blow up between Bedelia and my mother. She beat the hell out of my mother. If my Dad hadn't stepped in and stopped the fight she would have killed my mother. Before I learned about that I often wondered how my mother got those horrible scars on the left side of her neck and on her left arm. I guess it is true that scars from a razor cut never go away.

According to my grandmother things got worse after *the race* began. Bedelia and my mother tried to beat one another out as far as having babies by my Dad was concerned. However, Bedelia had more sense than my mother did and at least at the time she was married to him. She stopped having babies after number seven between her and my Dad was born. My grandfather had to stop Mama because she showed no signs of stopping or even wanting to.

After I was born he dragged my mother off to the first doctor he could find. One who would cut and tie her tubes for as little money as possible. Then he put a gun to my Dad's head and made him an offer he couldn't refuse. "Marry my daughter," he told my father angrily, "and give all those kids a name or lose your balls." Talk about a *shotgun* wedding. He and my grandmother were sick and tired of the whole sordid ordeal.

So my Dad divorced Bedelia and married my mother *after* having nine children by her. It must have been quite a task having all of our last names changed on our birth certificates. We never heard anything about our other siblings. But you can always depend on people to talk about a scandal like that in a small town like ours. From what we did hear my Dad and Bedelia had three girls and four boys together. We never saw any photographs of them or even knew their names which had to be on purpose. At some point in our lives we should have seen them, or at least heard their names yet we never did.

I don't think my mother cared to know anything about our other siblings. In fact, she acted like they didn't even exist. However, the day was coming when all that would change. My grandmother was always ready and willing to tell us about our parent's past. She could laugh about it by then. Although none of it was even remotely funny to her when it was going on.

I often wondered if my Dad thought about his other children. After he left her and filed for divorce Bedelia took them away and nobody knew where they went. Sometimes he would be sitting

alone and I would see tears in his eyes. I guess he was thinking about them and missing them.

My father was so handsome. He was tall, dark-complexioned and slender with dark hair and

dark eyes. His hair was beginning to gray a little as was my mother's even though they were

still fairly young. My brothers resembled our father and my sisters and I looked like Mama.

 My parents got as much financial support from my maternal grandparents as they could. They loved

us very much and were never afraid to show it. My father's parents were dead so we never knew them.

I don't know why but his family had not been big on taking photographs. Maybe it was the reason

why his brother, Arnet, loved a camera and snapping people's photographs so much. My Dad told

us that he took pictures of anything he could and I do mean anything.

My father's parents died while he was still a young boy. His two brothers, Caleb and Arnet,

were younger than he was. He had an older brother, Wayne, who lived a good distance

away from us so we rarely saw him. He was married but he and his wife never had any

children. I don't think she could have children from what I overheard. Yet, regardless of that

she and my uncle seemed to be happy together.

Uncle Wayne was much older than my Dad, Uncle Caleb and Uncle Arnet. So when their

parents died he stepped up to the plate and raised his three younger brothers. They knew of

no other family they ever had.

Uncle Caleb and Uncle Arnet didn't live far from us and worked at the steel plant as

Welders like my Dad. They were both married with children. Yet, there were no family

gatherings with my parents and my uncles. Their wives could not stand my mother so my

uncles would visit us without them. Even they didn't talk about our other siblings. My aunts treated me

and my siblings nice whenever we did see them, but asked us not to visit them. Just in case

Bedelia might decide to show up.

My grandparents believed that the day would come when my Dad would do to my mother what

he did to Bedelia. That and the fact that he was a poor man was the reason why they didn't

care very much for him in the beginning. Sadly, if that day would ever have come we would never

know.

My father was a hard working man yet he always had time for all of us. We would spend

hours playing all kinds of games in the evening before dinner. Our family ate dinner late in the

evenings. After that it was time to wash up and go to bed. A lot of people did things just the

opposite by having dinner much earlier. But that's how it was done in our house and we loved it.

Often I eaves-dropped on the hushed conversations between my mother and Gram Zela. My Dad

still took care of Bedelia and my other siblings. The court attached his wages at his request but

wouldn't tell him where they were. I believe my Dad knew where they were since my uncle's

wives were friends with Bedelia.

Through the conversations I overheard, my Dad not seeing his other children was

particularly hard on the youngest of his and Bedelia's children. It was a daughter. I couldn't stop

wondering why he chose to stay away from them. Maybe he was too ashamed to face them

because of my mother and us. It wasn't fair. We were just children. Innocent victims who had

absolutely nothing to do with what went on between my Dad, Mama and Bedelia. Deep down inside I

knew it was really because of Mama why he stayed away from them.

My grandparents weren't much better off financially than we were. Uncle Zane

and Uncle Whil tried to help us, too, but they had families of their own. Then Pop Berry developed a

bad case of Rheumatism in his left hip and had to stop working at the steel plant. He was there

for nearly fifty years. Gram Zela was getting too old for 'Day's Work' so both of them went on

Social Security. My grandfather received his full pension as well.

Pop Berry was ninety seven years old when he passed away. He and Gram Zela looked good

for their ages. My grandmother outlived him by thirteen years. I could've sworn I overheard

her tell someone that they were never really married. He already had a wife when

she met him. In the back of my mind I believed Gram Zela was a live-wire just like my mother

used to be when she was a young woman.

Things had turned around between my Dad and Pop Berry before my grandfather died. I

would hear them laughing and talking together when they were alone. They developed a deep

respect for each other and often joked about how my parents got together.

I wished I knew more about my other siblings. I seemed to be the only one who was

curious about them. I couldn't understand why my brothers and sisters were not as curious about them

as I was. Around the age of six I started to pay even closer attention to my mother's and Gram Zela's

conversations. By that time they were getting more interesting.

"I'm telling you, Anna," my grandmother said to Mama one day, "Joe will never have much

of anything. He has too many mouths to feed so you'd better keep a job." "Mom, please,"

replied Mama, "do I have to keep on hearing this?" "Sure you do," said Gram Zela incredulously.

"I always told you to keep your drawers up and your dress down didn't I?" "Joe and I know

what's on our plates," retorted Mama defending my father.

"Do you remember," began Gram Zela, "when you wore shoes with holes in the bottom of

them for over a month?" Mama didn't say anything. "It was after Damiz was born," continued

my grandmother. "You barely have shoes to wear now. It's a good thing we wear the same size.

You don't even own a decent dress. Joe doesn't have one suit to wear and neither do any of

the boys."

"Oh, Mom," said Mama with a touch of melancholy in her voice, "we'll make it. Believe me we'll get by." "You have to do more that just *get by*, Anna," Gram Zela said sarcastically. I could tell that she was as tired of having the same conversation with my mother as Mama was of hearing it.

"Tell me," continued my grandmother, "what would you do, Anna, if an occasion arose where you *had* to be nicely dressed? And not just you, daughter, but the children, too?" "Mom," replied my mother, "I don't want to talk about this. Okay? Joe and I love each other and our family. That's all there is to it. It doesn't matter what you say."

Nobody could've known that my grandmother's words would prove to be prophetic. An occasion was going to arise when all of us would need to be dressed nicely, or at least a little better than we usually were. It would be the worst occasion that any family had to face. Given themselves circumstances at the time we should have seen it coming. Then again who really wants to see something like that or even have any inkling about it? It was something that never should have happened. Something that still brings tears to my eyes and horror to my heart. I believe that somehow Mama did know. She knew that something was coming but just didn't know what it was. Maybe my Dad knew, too. It would be a horrifying tragedy for us to have to live through.

Chapter Two

We lived in a three bedroom house that stood all by itself on a small, dead-end

street. Most of the people in our area had big families and were just *getting by*. Yet, I don't think

any of them were as bad off as we were. For one thing my parents had more children than

anybody else did.

I can't tell you how hard it was to cope with having only one bathroom in the house. We

desperately needed a much bigger house and more than one bathroom. My parents put piss buckets

out at night. Nobody had a problem if they woke up during the night and had to use the bathroom.

Unless you were stumbling around in the dark and happened to accidentally knock one of them over.

My brothers shared a bedroom and my sisters and I shared one.

Everything I wore was handed down to me from Gina and Venna. I didn't know what it

felt like to have something new. Something that had only been mine and nobody else's.

Christmas for my siblings and I consisted of homemade stockings stuffed with some fruit and

a little bit of candy. If we got any toys at all it was because somebody donated them to us. For

years my parents managed to preserve the same artificial, silver Christmas tree that my Dad

found on the trash after my twin brothers were born.

My father spent most of that day in his bedroom. When and if he did come out there would be

sadness in his eyes. He loved all of us dearly but it was easy to guess that he missed

his other children. Still, he wouldn't talk about them.

Every day my mother had a big pot of food on the stove for us. We ate a lot of beans with little

meat and lots of rice. On Sunday we usually had fried chicken for dinner. It was always chicken

wings but we had fried chicken. For a long time I thought it was the only part of the bird

that people cooked. Mr. Bergon, who ran the grocery store nearby us, would let my mother have

a big bag of wings for $2.00. When I got older I found out that, along with the back of the chicken, it

was just another part of the bird that the stores threw away at that time. That big pot of food with the

rice on the side would still be on the stove for us.

Mr. Bergon was a kind, middle-aged man who felt sorry for our family. He was short, stout

and fair-skinned with sparkling, green eyes. He wasn't only nice to us but to many other poor

families in our area. He lost his wife and two daughters in a terrible fire. The store was closed

for a long time then suddenly it was all boarded up. We never knew what happened to him. He was

a wonderful man who suffered a terrible tragedy. I wondered why such a thing had happened to

him and how he would go on after that. It wouldn't be long before we would experience our own

tragedy and learn first-hand that people have no choice but to go on.

Two years later we saw his obituary in the local newspaper. He had been in and

out of the hospital with heart problems before he had a massive heart attack and died.

I don't think he ever got over the loss of his family. The newspaper was almost a month old when

I saw it. I recalled my parents being very sad around that time. And the night they left our

house for a while with many of our neighbors all dressed in black.

Mama would bake a cake or pie for us sometimes. It was always on the Sabbath Day. Some

of the neighbors would bring us food and baked goods, too. As poor as they were even many of them

felt sorry for us.

We managed to have two old television sets. One was in the living room and the other one was in my parent's bedroom. Both of them were given to us by my grandparents. No one in our area could afford to pay for cable television so we never saw it. That is, not until Miss Moble' moved into the house down the street from us.

Miss Larna Moble' was a sixty two year old, retired Seamstress. She lived with her two older sisters, Ellena and Fura, who were retired School Teachers. None of them had ever been married or had any children. They told us that they moved from the city to a small town to live a quiet, peaceful life. Harly was a quiet, peaceful town until a horrifying tragedy would change all of that.

The house they moved into had been empty since, Mrs. Sills, the previous owner passed away. She was a widow nearly ninety five years old when she died. She had no family so everybody on our street tried to look out for her. One night she went to sleep and never woke up. One of our neighbors went to look in on her when she hadn't been seen for two days. She was found still sitting in her favorite chair with a peaceful smile on her lips.

The Moble' sisters came around and introduced themselves to everybody. They brought homemade goodies with them. Everybody liked them immediately. Miss Larna was the most outgoing of the sisters. Ellena and Fura were friendly but more private. Miss Larna offered to make clothes for all of the children in the area whose parents couldn't afford to buy new clothes. All they had to do was provide her with the material.

All three of the Moble' sisters were nice looking women. Yet, we never saw any of them in the company of a man. There was plenty of speculation about that for a while. It died out fast, however, when the cable television truck was seen in front of their house. After that the Moble' sisters always had company at their house, men, women and children from the area.

It was only up until a certain time of the day that the women would receive visitors. You couldn't come to their house too early in the day or stay to late. They had to draw the line somewhere or they would've been overwhelmed with people every day.

Mama loved music and would listen to the portable radio in our kitchen. She couldn't carry a tune but she would try to sing along with the songs she liked. None of us could sing for that matter except my Dad. We heard him singing along with Mama one day and his voice was amazing. He had definitely missed his calling.

None of us will ever forget my Dad's deep, wonderful, baritone voice. We knew there were many great singing voices in the world. Voices that would never be heard and should have been. My father could have held his own with any super star alive. Why he never went down that road to stardom we will never know and we never thought to ask him.

Unknown to us at the time there was someone else who would do that for my Dad. I was too young to know how much children can alter your life and my father had sixteen of us. Sadly, our family couldn't afford a tape recorder. Because there is nothing I wouldn't give to hear my father sing again.

My mother seemed to be happiest when she was singing along with the songs on the radio. Many times she would start dancing to the music. Sometimes my parents had their own private party together right there in our kitchen. Years would pass before I understood that it was their 'escape'. They could let go of the pressures that were on them if only for a little while.

I didn't fully realize how the music they loved so much could do that for them. However, the day was coming when I understood it completely. That precious memory of my parents dancing and singing together in our kitchen always makes me smile. Not only that it never fails to bring tears to my eyes.

Chapter Three

My siblings and I attended the schools in our area. I was in the first grade when I began to fully understand what it meant to be poor. Mama had a unique ability for preserving our clothing. I thanked God that the other children in our school didn't have great memories where clothing was concerned. The clothes I wore to school had already been worn there over and over again for years before I got there.

Our school started to provide free lunches. You were only eligible if your family was too poor to pay. One day in the lunchroom my sister started talking to a friend of hers' who was in line with us. "I really hate this," said Gina. "I hate standing in the *'freebie'* line." Her friend didn't say anything. I guess it didn't bother her and it certainly didn't bother me either. You stood in the *'freebie'* line and ate, or you went hungry for the rest of the day until you got home. My sister stopped complaining. It didn't take long for her to realize that her pride wasn't worth starving for.

Although Gina and I got Venna's hand-me-downs what Venna got was never new. Mama practically lived in the thrift shops. Hardly any children from the better areas of town went to our school. The girls who did go there were used to having nice new things. So they never noticed that we were wearing some of their *old* things.

Angel, Devon and Lee were in high school and it was the same way for them. My brothers liked the girls but couldn't afford to date any of them. Angel and Devon had a big argument with our parents one night because they wanted to quit school and find jobs.

Zuroi and Aziel enlisted in the Military during their last year of high school. I thought that was foolish. They could have made it that last year and gotten their high school diplomas. But neither one of them could handle being flat broke anymore and never being able to do anything they wanted to do. My Dad was in the Marines when he was a young man so he was all for it. Mama never said much of anything about it. I guess because my Dad was happy for them she was, too.

My father could have easily gotten Angel and Devon jobs at the steel plant. But during that past year the bosses wanted all new employees to have a high school diploma. My brothers had no choice. They had to stay in school and graduate for any kind of chance at a decent job.

There was one girl that Devon liked a lot. Her name was, Patsie Pierce. She lived in a much nicer area of Harly and went to a better school. Patsie was a Sophomore like Devon was. They met at a basketball game one evening between their school teams. She convinced her parents after that to transfer her to Devon's school not mentioning him of course.

Patsie never told her parents the entire reason for her wanting to change schools. She told us they assumed it was because she wanted to get as far away as possible from her ex-boyfriend. He wasn't taking the break up between them well and had started stalking her. It was creeping her out. Patsie was a very pretty girl and nice. She had already broken up with this guy whose name was, Hallie, when she met Devon.

Hallie Juxon was a Junior at Patsie's old school. She told us he was too jealous and possessive for her and regretted the day that she met him. It was in her best interest to get rid of him, she thought, before he started acting crazier than he already was. Patsie confided in us that she believed he was dangerous. I couldn't get my mind around that. By the time we found out how right she was about Hallie it was too late.

Our neighbor, Mrs. Walford, let Devon use her telephone in the evening for an hour or so to talk to Patsie. She was a kind, middle-aged lady whom we could tell was lonely. She never had any children and her husband was rarely at home. We overheard Gram Zela and Mama talking about the young woman he was sneaking around with across town. From what we could hear this woman had two children by Mrs. Walford's husband. Mrs. Walford was still fairly good looking. She was short, stout but shapely with dark-brown hair, hazel eyes and fair skin. She had two tomcats, Barry and Daveed, that she treated like children.

Our parents taught us to always repay a kindness. Therefore, in return for allowing him to use her telephone Devon kept Mrs. Walford's lawn mowed and manicured. My brother wouldn't have asked her for any money but she insisted on paying him. It wasn't much and our family needed every penny we could get our hands on. It wasn't hard to know that Mrs. Walford felt as sorry for us as everyone else who lived around us did.

Patsie would telephone Devon at Mrs. Walford's house. Our neighbor would come to her back porch and call for Devon whenever she called for him. I'm sure she was happy to be an integral part of a budding romance.

Angel and Devon got after school jobs at one of the supermarkets. After a while they managed to save enough money to spend on themselves. Angel wasn't too interested in dating anyone. He loved reading comic books and the older they were the better. He was sure they would become valuable one day and collected a lot of them that people threw away.

Devon used some of his money to take Patsie to the movies once in a while. They liked hanging out with their friends, too. On one occasion they encountered a serious problem. Patsie's ex-boyfriend threatened her and Devon. My brother laughed it off as he told my family and I about the incident. I was glad that our parents were not at home at the time because we didn't think it was funny, and they wouldn't have either.

"You'd better be careful of that guy, Dev," Angel warned by brother. "There are a lot of fools out here and he sounds like one of them. Don't be too quick to write this Hallie guy and his threats off as nothing." Our parents never knew anything about Hallie's threats to Devon and Patsie because we never told them.   It was a mistake we would regret for the rest of our lives. They would have done something about Hallie Juxon and his threats. To this day I feel somewhat responsible for what happened in the end and I'm not alone.

Our family liked Patsie. She never looked down her nose at anybody. And she was at our house so much you would have thought she lived there, too. Patsie was tall, skinny with a lovely face, big, dark eyes, long, thick, dark hair and a fair complexion. She dressed nicely, too. Her father left her mother for another woman when she was eight years old. The woman, to our shock, was her mother's sister. A year later he divorced Patsie's mother and married her. I could tell that Patsie and her mother were still bitter by the way she talked to us about it.

Patsie's parents, Lelia and Eric Pierce, shared custody of her. She was an only child. She spent summers with her Dad and her step-mother/aunt, Barbra. Barbra had four children who were all teenagers and had different fathers. She had never been married until Patsie's father. Patsie was now old enough to decide where she wanted to be during the summer. She didn't think she would be spending summers with her Dad anymore. She loved him but didn't care much for Barbra after what happened. The tension in the home was getting to everybody as Patsie got older.

Eric Pierce owned a lucrative chain of auto parts stores. Lelia was a stay-at-home Mom by choice. She had a college degree in Music and was thinking of taking a teaching position in one of the schools in Harly. Patsie's parents liked Devon, however, they didn't want him with

Patsie. I'm sure I don't have to tell you why. My family and I knew there were people in the

world who thought they were better than others. In their eyes my brother was too poor for their

daughter. But for the Grace of God they could have been in our place.

I thanked God that Patsie was nothing like her parents. Yet, they felt just the

opposite way about Hallie Juxon. We heard that his family was well-to-do. They had to be aware

of his abusive treatment toward Patsie. I began to feel sorry for Eric and Lelia because they were so

short-sighted and shallow.

Patsie and Devon became one of the most popular couples in their school. The whole

student body liked them. As their relationship started to grow so did Hallie's threats toward

them. I could have understood if he was some fat, ugly guy who couldn't get a girlfriend. When

I saw him I was stunned. He was one of the most good looking guys I had ever seen. Sadly,

he desperately needed emotional help. The people who should have seen that he had serious

mental issues were his parents. They were the closest people to him.

I found out that Hallie's family did know he had problems but chose to ignore it. Maybe they

thought his problems would just miraculously vanish. Yet, as he got older his problems grew worse. It

was just a matter of time before he hurt somebody, or himself. He had problems ever since he was a

child. Every pet the family had always turned up dead somewhere in their house. A kitten his mother

got for him was found with its' throat cut the day after she gave it to him. How can any parent ignore

things like that?

It wasn't long before the Sophomore Dance was coming up at Patsie's and Devon's high school.

They were very excited about it as they made plans to go. It was all any of the teenagers in our area

could talk about, even the ones who didn't go to that school. Our family was as excited about the

Dance as Devon and Patsie were.

Patsie was like another sister to my siblings and I. We grew to love her very much and we knew she loved us. She was an easy person to love and the most altruistic person we would ever meet, up to that point in our lives. We were certain she would become a permanent part of our family one day. Yet, because of the uncertainty about anything in life we would never see that happen.

Chapter Four

It was the night of the Sophomore Dance. Patsie and Devon looked fantastic. She brought her

camera and took lots of pictures. I will always be thankful to God for that. It was a joyous

time and something we would always remember. A wonderful shining light had enveloped us before

a horrifying darkness came that would consume us.

Before Devon and Patsie left to go to the Dance all of us sat around laughing and talking

together. It was as if we wanted to talk more to each other that night than we usually did. As we

looked at the clock on the wall the Dance would be starting in an hour. It was a warm,

beautiful, starry night that was magical.

My Dad turned on the television in the living room while the rest of us sat in the kitchen. After

that he went upstairs to get ready to take Devon and Patsie to the Dance. Mama went outside to

talk to some of our neighbors. Mrs. Walford and the Moble' sisters were making a big fuss over how

great my brother and Patsie looked.

From the kitchen we could hear a musical Talent Show that was airing on television. While we

listened we heard the beautiful, deep, soulful voice of a young girl singing on the show. We had heard

her on the radio before but couldn't recall her name. No one got up to see what the girl on

the television show looked like. We just listened.

"Wow," exclaimed Venna when the song was over, "who is that?" "Oh," replied Patsie, "that was

Corinne something. I can't remember her last name." "Who?" asked Lee. "I can understand," began

Patsie, "why you guys haven't heard of her yet. She's just coming onto the music scene. You still should've heard of her though." "I think I've heard of her," said Lee. "I figured she must be new." Then Patsie looked at Devon smiling.

"Dev," said Patsie, "your family hasn't heard of that girl, Corinne, that sings." "They don't listen to the radio that much," replied Devon, "but Mama does. I'll bet she's heard of her." "Well," Patsie told us, "she's on her way to becoming a great female singer. If she makes singing her career I wouldn't be surprised if one day she won't be one of the greatest singers of all time. Right now she's only around thirteen or fourteen years old. So she's too young to be signed to a contract with anybody."

"With a voice like that," replied Venna, "there is no way they'll let her get away. You know how those money-grubbers in the music business are." "I'm sure," said Angel matter of factly, "there's an adult around somewhere to protect that girl."

When my Dad came back downstairs another singer was displaying their talent on the program. He went outside to join my mother and our neighbors. A few minutes later the rest of us went outside. As we stood around Patsie turned the conversation back to Caron Cato.

"I feel kind of sad for that girl, Corinne," said Patsie solemnly. "Why?" asked Gina curiously. "Well," began Patsie, "I read in an interview that she doesn't think she will ever get the kind of song she really wants. The kind that tells people what is truly in your heart and soul. It has something to do with her father." "What happened to him?" asked Angel. "All I've heard," answered Patsie, "is that she lost him from her life some years ago." "He's dead?" Lee asked in shock. "No," replied Patsie. "Something happened between her parents and they split up." "With a voice like that," said Venna, "she shouldn't have a problem getting what she wants." "I hope you're right," replied Patsie.

"A lot of singers," said Angel, "have to be out there for a long time before they get a break." "I know," said Gina. "But all they need is that one bullet and pow they're on top of the charts."

I started to wonder what Corinne's life must have been like. What it must be like to be on

your way to becoming a big celebrity.

I didn't listen to the radio like Mama did and I didn't have a favorite song or favorite

singer either. Yet, somehow I knew that one day I would be a huge fan of Corinne's music. Over the

years I didn't know I would grow to love her music more and more. Although I knew hardly anything

about her I felt a connection with her that I couldn't explain. There was something in her voice that

touched my spirit like no other singer I heard ever did, or would.

Around seven forty five my Dad got Devon, Patsie and himself into our old station wagon and they

headed for the Dance. He was going back at midnight to pick them up when it was over. Then he would

drive Patsie home and come home with Devon. Mama was letting all of us stay up and watch television

that night until Devon came home. All of us were anxious to hear about the nice time he and Patsie

had at the Dance.

Around eleven forty five my Dad got the car keys and headed for the front door. He was going to get

Devon and Patsie from the Dance. "We'll see you when you get home with Devon, Joe," my mother

said to my father smiling tenderly. Then something strange happened.

I caught a long, loving look between my parents as they smiled at each other. There was

something in their eyes that I never saw before. It was as if they were seeing each

other for the last time. I couldn't have known how right I was. I watched my Dad as he left the

house, got into the car and drive off.

As we watched television all of us dozed off to sleep. I awakened first and saw nothing but snow on

the screen. Quietly, I got up and went into the kitchen to look at the clock on the wall. I was surprised

when I saw that it was two o'clock in the morning. *"Maybe Dad and Devon came home,"* I thought,

"and just didn't bother to wake us up." I went back into the living room and gently shook Mama

awake. "Oh, my," she said groggily sitting up in her chair. "What time is it, Zo?" I told her what

time it was.

"What?" she cried in surprise. "My, Lord, we've been asleep all this time? Where's your

Dad and Devon?" My father and brother were not home yet. As we talked the others slowly

awakened. Suddenly, for no logical reason a photograph of my Dad slid off the wall and hit the floor.

No one went near it as we stood there for about ten seconds just staring at it. That picture had

hung there securely for years. There was no reason in the world for it to fall off the wall like

it did. I watched as Mama turned pale. Something was wrong and she knew it.

Mama slowly walked over, picked up the picture and put it back on the wall. We noticed that her

hands were trembling slightly. "I-I h-hope nothing happened with the car," she said nervously as

she grabbed her sweater and put it around her shoulders. She knew as well as we did that if something

had happened with the car we would have known about it long before then. Mama hurried next door to

Mrs. Walford's house. My siblings and I nervously waited for her to return home. As we did there was

a knock on our front door. When my sister, Gina, opened it two Police Officers were standing there.

They asked for my mother. The look on their faces was not a happy one.

Through the open door, as we stood behind Gina, we could see my mother hurriedly

approaching the two officers. Mrs. Walford was with her. The officers pulled my mother aside. We

knew something had happened and it wasn't good.

We watched as Mrs. Walford put her arms around my mother's shoulders and the officers walked

away shaking their heads. Mama's entire countenance fell as she and our neighbor came into our house.

There was a look on my mother's face I had never seen before and hope I never see again. Her whole

world collapsed around her and ours did, too. It was Mrs. Walford who told us what happened. And

explained the look of sheer shock and disbelief that was on Mama's face.

My mother was numb as she stared into space like she was in a trance. Mrs. Walford had tears in her eyes as she talked to us. Five days, six hours, twelve minutes and eight seconds would pass before Mama uttered another sound. It would be the sound of her heart-wrenching, guttural sobs at the double funeral for my Dad and Devon. We were devastated. It didn't get any better for us since our family, except for Mama, would attend Patsie's funeral six days later.

 On the night of the Sophomore Dance, after my father and Devon hadn't come home, Mama telephoned, Lelia, Patsie's mother. Patsie hadn't come home either. When Lelia hadn't heard from my Dad, Devon or Patsie she called the police. The police already knew about the terrible tragedy that occurred at the Dance. They just hadn't gotten around to notifying us yet.

My father and brother were killed instantly. However, Patsie held on longer than expected before she slipped into a coma and never woke up. She had lost a lot of blood and suffered horrific internal injury. They put her on life support until her parents were informed that she was brain dead and there was no hope. We will always admire her strength and courage. Because before she slipped into that coma, and barely able to talk, she was determined to tell the Police what happened. Also, there were several witnesses who saw everything.

The Dance was over when my Dad arrived there to pick up Devon and Patsie that night. No one was coming out of the building. After waiting for fifteen minutes my Dad went inside to see what was going on. He heard loud, angry quarreling when he entered the auditorium where the Dance was being held. He made his way through a crowd of spectators. The argument was between Devon, Patsie and Hallie Juxon. Hallie shouldn't have been there in the first place.

The Chaperons were trying to get things under control so people could leave with no trouble. Finally they had no choice but to threaten Hallie with calling the police on him. When he heard that he quickly left only to return just before the Dance was over. He had been stalking Devon and Patsie for a while. Patsie told us how upset my Dad was with her and Devon. When he got involved in the argument Hallie left again.

"What's this nonsense all about you two?" my Dad wanted to know from Devon and Patsie. "I came here to pick you up thinking you had a good time and I walk into this? All hell is breaking loose." "It's nothing, Dad," Devon told my father. "That stupid jerk won't leave us alone, Mr. Moran," Patsie told my Dad almost in tears. "Alright," my father told them, "let's just get out of here."

The three of them went outside and got into the car to come home. People began to leave the building at that time, too. While they were inside the car my Dad was still very upset with her and Devon.

"That guy threatened you two before," said my Dad in disbelief, "and you didn't say anything?" "Yeah, Dad," answered Devon. "He's crazy so don't worry about it." "I don't like this, Dev," my Dad told him. "You should have told us about this. Come Monday morning we're getting a Restraining Order against that fool for you both. I don't understand why your mother hasn't done that already, Patsie." Patsie never told her parents just how bad things had really gotten with Hallie.

"Don't worry about it, Dad," Devon kept telling my father. "People are crazy out here, son," my Dad warned him. "You can't take any chances."

At the Dance Hallie kept trying to pick a fight with Devon. The more Devon ignored him the angrier he got. Patsie and Devon informed the Chaperons about what was going on. They had to throw Hallie out of the building twice but he would manage to sneak back in. Of course he was blasted, probably on drugs and alcohol. He was determined that if he couldn't have Patsie no one else would. As she was telling everything she couldn't stop

apologizing but no one ever blamed her. We never knew Hallie pulled a gun on her and Devon

once either.

My Dad calmed down and started the car to drive home. He, Devon and Patsie were sitting in the

front seat. Hallie stood in front of the car with a sawed off shot gun in his hands. People started

screaming. Patsie talked about a great flash of light that blinded them and then there was

a horrible blast. After that everything went black for her.

The police took us to see our station wagon. The front of it was completely destroyed as if it

had collided head on into another car. The windshield was gone. Hallie Arnold Juxon who was

eighteen years old and left back twice in the eleventh grade was arrested at his home two hours

later. After telling all that happened Patsie Pierce went to sleep forever.

My family had no life insurance money to bury my Dad and Devon. My Dad's job

provided a little insurance money but it was nowhere near enough. So our neighbors went

from door to door collecting money for us. The two newspapers in Harly solicited money for our

family, too. We were God-fearing people but rarely went to church. Still, the Methodist church offered

to have the double funeral there. It was a fairly big church and a good thing it was. There were so

many people at the funeral many of them had nowhere to sit. Some people couldn't even get inside the

building.

The tragedy was all over the news for a long time. Our family received over $50,000.00 which

was more than enough to cover the burials and a nice headstone. What wasn't spent on funeral

expenses my mother used for our survival during the following months.

For viciously and savagely murdering my father, my brother and Patsie in cold blood Hallie

was tried a year later. Unfortunately, he was found not guilty by reason of insanity. We wanted to see him to get the death penalty. Instead he would spend the rest of his life in an institution for the criminally insane. It was more than obvious that his family's money kept him off Death Row. Nothing they did to him would've brought our loved ones back. The wonderful love we could have shared with them for years to come was snatched away from us. All because of something utterly senseless. It's a terrible thing when we have to bury our dearly loved ones. The old axiom that says, *'Time heals all wounds'* is not true. At least not for us, and not for any parent who has had to bury a child.

Zuroi and Aziel were home with us for a month before they had to return to base. They promised to keep sending Mama money to help out. On the day they left us a sorrowful feeling filled my heart. I knew it would be a long time before we would see them again. Because of what happened to my father and Devon our house would never again be home for my oldest brothers. Their visits to see us became more infrequent over the years.

I read a letter that Zuroi wrote to Mama six months after the tragedy. He and Aziel were requesting to be housed on a Military base in a city that was 2,000 miles away. When their Military service was over they planned to make their permanent home there.

Lelia never got over Patsie's death. She never looked very well at the trial. Two weeks after Hallie's sentencing a friend became concerned for her. So she decided to pay Lelia a visit since she couldn't get her on the telephone. She found Lelia hanging from the ceiling in Patsie's bedroom. A lock of Patsie's baby hair was clutched in one of her hands. According to the Coroner she had been hanging there for at least three days. It wasn't hard to know that she had carried some guilt over what happened to daughter, Devon and my Dad. She just couldn't live with it any longer.

Chapter Five

It wasn't long before our family was struggling financially again. Mama knew she had to do

something. For a long time she couldn't seem to get her head or her heart together. She got my

father's pension money and social security for herself and us but more was needed. Refusing

to go to the County for help she tried to take on more 'Days Work'.

Mama took one day off and that was Sunday. She would leave for work every morning at the crack

of dawn. It was late at night when she got home so we hardly saw her. My mother never had

a real chance to grieve. She couldn't afford to take any time off. She had the responsibility of

supporting herself and six children, and dead set against any of us quitting school to help her.

Sunday was the one day of the week that our family would spent together. But after the deaths of

my Dad and Devon that changed. Now on Sunday all Mama did was sleep because she was so

tired. Yet, she would get up long enough to cook that pot of food for us. During the week she would

prepare a pot of food at night when she came home from work. All Angel had to do was take

it out of the refrigerator and heat it up for us on the following evening. He was the one who

looked after us while Mama worked. Also, he still had his job at the supermarket after school.

My brother loved helping my mother in any way that he could.

Angel always got good grades in school. We were so proud of him when he won one of three

full scholarships. One of them was to a prestigious technical college on the East coast beginning in the

Fall. He wanted to do something in Computer Graphics and did his best to explain to us what storyboarding was. He couldn't wait to get to college. We knew he would do well in life and make all

of us proud, especially Mama. Nobody could have guessed that our joy would be short lived.

It was no surprise when Mama suddenly fell ill. Usually by the time Angel awakened us for school

my mother was long gone for work. One particular morning we got up and she was still in bed. When

Angel tried to awaken her she wouldn't wake up. Lee ran next door to Mrs. Walford's house and called

for an ambulance. When the Paramedics arrived they performed CPR on my mother immediately. My

siblings and I began to sob as we watched them put her into the ambulance and drive away. We

thought my mother was going to die and we would be orphans.

At the hospital the doctors informed us that Mama had suffered a mild heart attack in her

sleep. My Dad's job had provided health insurance for our family. However, when he passed

away so did the insurance. Mama received the best possible care. Imagine our surprise when we

found out that two days before she got sick she swallowed her pride and went to the County for help.

She got medical assistance for herself and for us. It was as if she knew that something was going to

happen to her. It couldn't have been a coincidence. There was no way to explain the timing for her

sudden change of heart.

I recalled the night that my Dad and Devon were murdered and the strange look between my

parents. Also, how my Dad's picture mysteriously fell off the wall, and my mother's trembling

hands when she picked it up and put it back. I believed that there was a strong possibility that Mama

could sense or 'see' things. It's eerie how you never notice things about the people you love until you

get older. Mama stayed in the hospital for two weeks. At least she was finally getting the rest she so

desperately needed for her mind as well as her body.

Chapter Six

Mama had managed to put aside a little bit of money from her work. Yet, by the time she came home from the hospital and got back on her feet it was all gone. The doctors made one thing clear to her and to us that she was no longer able to work. They gave her medicine for her heart and made a way for her to get it for free since it was so expensive. I don't think anybody realized it at first except me. But no doctor would ever be able to heal my mother's broken heart. There was no medicine that had ever been invented for that.

Mama was always paid under the table when she worked. However, she was able to get a little money from Social Security. It was a miracle that none of the utilities in our house were shut off and the rent was paid on time. We had God to thank for that.

Angel's boss, Mr. Buller, gave him food from the market where he worked to bring home for us. We were grateful for his kindness. Maxwell Buller was a little older than my Dad was. He and his wife, Sare, had three sons who were married with families of their own. Max and Sare looked like they could be brother and sister and there were plenty of rumors to that affect all over Harly. Both of them were short, stout, fair-complexioned with dark hair and dark eyes. They even talked alike. It was easy to see how much they loved each other.

Although things gradually got a little better for us the inevitable came. It made all of us sad especially Mama. She had worked so hard to stop it but some things are totally out of our control. Angel had to turn down the scholarship he won. Mama couldn't seem to stop crying about it. Deep down I think she felt it was her fault. It didn't matter how much my brother assured her otherwise. It made Angel want to take care of her and us all the more.

Contrary to what people may believe opportunity does knock more than once. Ever since we could understand our parents they drilled one thing into our heads. Only two things were important in life, God and family, in that order. Everything else was only clutter.

Angel graduated from high school with honors. He was given a promotion at work as Mr. Buller's Assistant Manager. The job came with a much better salary, too. With that and the money Mama got we were able to see some light at the end of a dark tunnel. Almost a year after that Angel gave Lee a part time job at the market and Venna started taking on jobs baby-sitting. Since her and Lee were teenagers Mama told them to keep their money for themselves.

Lee and Venna soon discovered what the stores meant by 'lay-away'. They patiently chipped away at whatever they owed on an item until it was theirs. You would've thought my sister found a gold mine on the day she brought home her first brand new outfit. She was so excited and mine and Gina's eyes sparkled. We knew that sooner or later the outfit would be ours.

For the next two years things moved for us at a slow and steady pace. Then, out of the blue, Angel stunned us by getting married. None of us saw that coming. We didn't even know my brother was dating anyone. Mama didn't seem to be the least bit surprised. I couldn't understand why I kept forgetting to ask Gram Zela about my mother *knowing* things.

Angel's new bride's name was, Helena. She was fair-skinned, tall with gray eyes and dark-brown brown hair. At first she was a little shy around us but eventually she came around.

Helena James' family was almost as poor as ours was. She was one of thirteen children and the oldest of four girls. She was only sixteen years old when her parents married her off to my brother. He was twenty. Mama would never have signed for Angel to get married to anybody so he never told us about it until it was done. Helena's parents were the ones who arranged everything. It was common practice for some poor families to lighten their burden by marrying off the older girls in the household as soon as it was appropriate. Helena screwed around a lot and everybody in town knew it. Unfortunately, Angel was the one who ended up getting her pregnant.

Angel fixed up the basement in our house for him and Helena. Mama didn't have to worry in case the twins decided to visit and needed somewhere to stay. In their letters Zuroi and Aziel told us they were traveling around the world. Then at last we were able to afford our own telephone and my brothers were able to call us once in a while.

By the time I was thirteen years old Angel and Helena were separated and in the process of getting one of those low-cost divorces. They agreed to share custody of their three children. My nephew, Jamesy, was four years old. My niece, Dara Lee, was three and the youngest, Mickey, was a year old. Angel was always working so the children spent a lot of time with Mama, Venna, Gina, Damiz and me when he was to have them. Needless to say, my brother vowed to never get married again.

Angel was twenty four years old, married, divorced and had three children. He hadn't mentioned Computer Graphics in a long time. Sadly, we realized he had given up on his dream. Sometimes I would catch Mama staring at him when he wasn't looking. I could see the tears well in her eyes. She never stopped blaming herself for the way things turned out for my brother.

Chapter Seven

After some time Mama seemed to get herself together. She started listening to the radio again and singing along with her favorite songs. I recalled my father's beautiful voice singing along with hers and my eyes would well with tears. My siblings and I made fun of Mama's singing but she didn't care and laughed right along with us. It was so good to hear her laugh again. Then there were times when she quietly sat at the kitchen table looking out of the window. It wasn't hard to know that she was thinking about my Dad and Devon.

In the meantime were hearing more about the young girl we heard singing on television that night long ago. Corinne was now Caron Cato and her star was on the rise in the entertainment world. She had one hit record after another. There was talk in the show business world that she couldn't seem to get the one song she desperately wanted. I didn't understand what that was really all about. People thought it might be time for her to change Managers or maybe even song writers. It was eerie how a strange feeling came over me whenever I thought about her. It was a mystery that I couldn't explain. Long before we actually met each other it was like I already knew her.

Things were going well for our family when Angel introduced us to a nice young lady he said that he liked a lot. She had just started working as a Cashier at the market where he worked. Her name was, Minda Banger, and she became like another member of our family. She was cute, short and a little on the plump side with short, dark-red hair, big blue eyes and dark skin. Minda told us she had been working at various jobs until she found her dream job. She wanted to work in show business, namely at something in the music industry, but she couldn't sing.

Angel and Minda were seeing each other for four months when she landed a job as an

Assistant to a well known Concert Promoter. One evening she and Angel brought the guy to

our house so we could meet him. Little did we know that Minda's new job would bring some

totally unexpected changes into our lives.

Rosco Morrison was nicknamed, 'King R', by others who worked with him in the

entertainment world. Supposedly because he was good at discovering great talent. He was in

his early forties, tall, dark, handsome, well-dressed and outgoing. We felt very comfortable with him

and vice versa. With Minda having a job like that we thought Angel had hit the jackpot. However, soon

after we met Rosco she and Angel parted ways but still remained friends. I'll never forget the

day when she offered to introduce us to Caron Cato. It was the catalyst to many revelations to come

for us, especially for me.

Minda got back stage passes for all of us to one of Caron's concerts but only Mama, Angel and I

were able to go. On the night of the event I could barely contain myself. Soon enough we were

standing back stage face to face with Caron herself.

I felt an instant connection with Caron and Angel felt the same way. She seemed so familiar

to us. It was as if we had known her all of our lives. My mother didn't feel quite the same way

that we did. She was happy to meet Caron but as we talked with her my mother seemed to

grow a little distant toward her. We had no idea at the time why she started acting that way.

Caron was medium-height like me. I missed being classified as tall by a half an inch.

Also, she had a gigantic voice. When she sang she hit one note after the other with unbelievable

ease. Her voice was bluesy and gritty. I couldn't help thinking about my Dad when I heard her sing.

Both of their voices were stunningly soulful. Caron had long dark hair that was braided on one side.

It was only one of the many different ways that she would fix her hair. Her eyes and her complexion were similar to mine and my siblings.

It was easy to see that Caron was fond of mid-riffs and stiletto heels. She told us that her favorite color was black and she liked rhinestones. Black was also my favorite color and I always had a preference for anything with rhinestones on it. All of Caron's concerts were always sold out and held in enormous arenas. Although she was a super star I saw sadness in her eyes. As we talked with her I found out that we shared the same kind of sadness.

"Are you the only singer in your family, Caron?" my mother wanted to know. "I am now," replied Caron sadly. "My father had a great voice and used to sing to us all of the time, but he died a long time ago." There was so much pain in her voice when she talked about her father. "Was he sick?" Angel wanted to know. "He was murdered," said Caron flatly. "Oh no," said Mama. "We're so sorry to hear that, honey. What happened?"

Caron's eyes welled with tears as she looked at us. "Oh," she replied, "some crazy kid shot him to death." We were stunned. I realized immediately that that must have been the connection I always felt with Caron. "I'm so sorry, Caron," Mama said again. A strange look came upon my mother's face. It was as if she suddenly thought of something that she couldn't share with the rest of us. She got very quiet after that.

"Damn," said Angel, "that's what happened to our father, too." "It really hurts," said Caron sorrowfully, "doesn't it?" My brother and I just nodded our heads. A lone tear spilled onto Caron's cheek that she wiped away. She was in so much pain over her father's death. Angel and I realized that we were still in a lot of pain over our own tragedy as well. Caron wiped another tear away.

"Well," said Caron, "I've got to go now but I sure hope I get to see you guys again." She took mine and Angel's hands in hers looking deeply into our eyes. "Yeah," said Mama almost in a whisper as we turned to leave. I could see that her mind was going a mile a minute suddenly.

We didn't know that she knew something that Angel and I didn't know. Caron went on stage as we took

our seats in the front row of the arena.

Caron was a fantastic performer. Her voice was so powerful she barely needed a microphone.

She had tremendous energy, too. From watching her show no one would ever guess how sad she

really was. People loved her. When her show was over she received a long standing ovation and

the people cried out for more. There were flashing lights coming from everywhere in the building.

After the show everyone was trembling just as we were from the excitement of Caron's performance

and they raved about it.

Reporters and television crews were inside the building as well as outside. They were talking

about Caron's show and asking where she was headed next. A stage hand had seen us talking with

her back stage. At her request he lead us toward the back of the building to avoid the crowd.

We had a great time or should I say Angel and I did. If Mama did you wouldn't have known it.

She didn't say two words and seemed to be glad we were leaving. I was curious to know what

was on her mind but I never asked her. I was young but not stupid. It doesn't matter what

dark secrets people try to hide. Sooner or later they are coming to the light. All you have

to do is wait.

As we were leaving the building we overheard a heated argument between a man and a

woman. We recognized the woman's voice as Caron's but couldn't recognize the man's voice.

From the stage hand we learned that the man was Caron's Manager and boyfriend, Zane Mattox.

I didn't see her for a long time after that. So I didn't think she would remember us but she did.

Years later I thought I would see Caron again back stage at another one of her concerts.

And, again it would be courtesy of Minda after she and Angel would start seeing each other again. Although Minda played a big part in that it wouldn't happen that way at all.

Remembering the night I first met Caron always made me smile. We may have been poor but now we knew a big celebrity. Caron was such a sweet, kind person and seemed to be a little partial to me. I paid no real attention to that at the time and hind-sight is twenty/twenty like people say. I started following her career.

Recalling Caron's deep sadness over her father's death kept me mindful of my own pain. It was like a personal emptiness that both of us shared. Each of us had lost someone very dear to us in a horrible way. Someone that we could never get back. A father who was stolen from our lives. I felt my own heartache again the moment Caron touched my hand and believed it must have been the same for Angel.

I began to feel something else that I hadn't felt in a long time. It was a feeling of peace and comfort. Thoughts of Caron comforted me and I hoped she felt the same way about us. I slept like a baby on the night after our first meeting. When I had not slept that well since before my Dad's and Devon's murders. Meeting Caron had a lot to do with that, yet at the time I didn't understand why.

Lee and Venna decided to leave home and move in with Gram Zela. My grandmother was lonely after Pop Berry died. Mama didn't mind when she asked if my brother and sister could come to live with her. Venna was out of school and working as a Secretary in one of the banks in Harly. Lee started working at the steel plant while going to city college part time. He wanted a career as an Accountant since he loved working with numbers. Neither one of them wanted to get married and we didn't have to guess why. Angel's marriage helped to turn all of us against that institution. Both Venna and Lee helped Mama financially.

Gina was in love with a man who was fifteen years older than she was. His name was, Jess Ross. He was handsome, tall, had money and was single. Jess was what we called a

Sugar Daddy to my sister. He bought Gina lots of nice things. She moved into his Condo with him which upset my mother to no end. From the beginning she was totally against their relationship citing that Jess was too old for my sister. Some people have a lot of nerve.

Mama was 'old school'. You didn't live with a man unless you were married to him. I thought that was a bit hypocritical on her part. She may not have lived with my Dad out of wedlock but he did already have a wife and children when she started sneaking around with him. Not to mention all the babies that she was having by my father before Pop Berry had to put his foot down.

It didn't phase Gina one bit. She always did exactly what she wanted to do no matter what anybody thought or said about it. In that regard she was a lot like Mama.

Gina worked as a Teacher's Assistant in one of Harly's elementary schools. Jess told her that she never had to work anywhere if she didn't want to. He was a Superintendent at the lumber yard in Harly and had been there for over fifteen years.

Angel, Dami and I were the only ones still at home with Mama. Angel kept his room in the basement and Dami and I finally had bedrooms all to ourselves. Our family's financial situation was getting better. All of my older siblings aided us. Even Jess contributed money to our household because of Gina. Mama made it clear to him that he didn't have to do that but he insisted. Needless to say, it made Gina happy. She assured Mama that he wasn't subtly trying to buy her daughter. All during this wonderful progression in our family Caron was never far from my mind.

Chapter Eight

I was sixteen years old when strange things started happening to me in the house. And, I was the only one who knew something was going on out the ordinary in there. My father and Devon had been dead for nine years and we missed them terribly. It began on a Saturday afternoon and I was at home alone. We had gotten another television set for the living room because the previous one stopped working. I was watching a favorite dance show that I liked. When intermission time came on I went upstairs to the bathroom.

While I was in the bathroom I noticed how everything suddenly got quiet downstairs. You could hear a pin drop. When I went back downstairs to the living room I saw that the television set was turned off. It was eery and I got a little scared. A chill ran down my spine when I could feel someone watching me. The hairs on my forearms and the back of my neck stood on end. My hand was shaking as I turned the television set back on then sat down on the sofa.

About fifteen minutes later I decided to go into the kitchen and make myself a snack. As I was putting peanut butter onto some crackers it got quiet in the living room again. Cautiously and slowly I walked back into the living room and saw that the television set was turned off again. A knot of panic crept into the pit of my stomach and I started trembling. I knew that something wasn't right. The television set surely couldn't turn itself off. Although I saw no one else there I could sense with certainty that *somebody* was in the room with me.

I began shaking so badly I could hardly move my legs as I quickly headed for the front door.

I was beyond scared as I saw Dami walking up the front stoop. I opened the door and greeted him nervously. He could easily see that something was wrong with me as his smile turned to a frown. "What's the matter with you, Zo?" he asked me concerned. I told him what happened to me while I was in the house. Needless to say, he didn't believe me.

"Oh, get out of here, Zo," Dami said chuckling a little. "Somebody was in there with me, Dami," I said to him upset. "Oh yeah," he replied snidely. "Who was it?" "I-I don't know," I told him shakily. "I-I couldn't see anybody b-but I know someone was in there." Dami smirked at me. "You mean," he said, "like a ghost?" "I don't care if you believe me or not," I said. "It didn't happen to you." I couldn't stop shaking.

"Alright," said Dami still grinning at me, "let's try a little experiment shall we?" "Like what?" I wanted to know. We went into the living room. Dami turned the television set on then we went outside to the backyard for a few minutes. When we came back into the living room the television was still on. Dami looked at me and smiled sarcastically. "There's nobody in here but us, Zo," he said. I looked at him wide eyed and still scared.

"Somebody was in here, Dami," I insisted as I slowly began to calm down. "I don't care if you believe me. I know what happened. Do you really think I would make up something like that up?" Dami chuckled softly again. "Just take it easy, Zo," he said as he headed upstairs. I stared at him. Then he stopped in the middle of the staircase and turned to me. "Tell me something, Zo," he said. "What?" I answered. "When are you going to learn how to dress?" I knew he was changing the subject so I didn't answer him. Instead I sat down on the couch and he continued up the stairs. I wasn't losing my mind and the way I dressed had nothing to do with what happened.

Dami was always on my case about my having no fashion sense. It was something my whole family joked about with me. What my brother was trying to do was get my mind on something else but it didn't work.

I never mentioned my chilling experience to anybody else in the family and neither did Dami. It was the beginning of a long series of strange, eerie occurrences to come. Things that only happened to me when I was alone in the house. Eventually they didn't only happen when I was at home but in other places as well. I would be in the girls' bathroom at school and thought I saw someone standing behind me when I looked in the mirror. There would be nobody in the bathroom at the time but me. I felt so alone for a long time because nothing was happening to anyone else in my family. I figured if I told anybody about it, like Dami, they wouldn't believe me. Yet, someone was coming into my life that I *would* be able to talk to about those things. And it was a very unlikely person.

Chapter Nine

I was a Junior at Zachary Eisenman Senior High School and had a fairly high I.Q. I

didn't have a boyfriend and was somewhat of a loner. There was no boy in school that I

wanted to be bothered with anyway. However, I became friendly with two boys in my Homeroom

class and a girl in my Spanish class. The latter person was quite by accident.

Preston Miarty and Roy Morgan were both sixteen years old like me. Those who were part of

our student body considered both of them to be computer whizzes. They would take a computer apart

piece by piece. Then put it back together again just for fun while timing themselves doing it.

Preston got into a lot of trouble because of his computer savvy.

 One night he was online and accidentally hacked into some classified information about a

man who worked for the Central Intelligence Agency. The authorities traced the out-going, personal

data right to his house while he was still on the computer. He and his whole family were taken

into custody. After a few hours of questioning they were released but his computer was

confiscated and never returned to him. They threatened Preston and informed him that

he would be watched for an indefinite period of time. It may only have been a ploy to scare him

but it worked. He stayed away from computers for a very long time and so did Roy.

Roy was more laid back and considered by other students to be cool. Both he and Preston

were well liked by everybody who knew them. They were handsome as well as smart.

The two guys had been friends since the first grade and lived right next door to each other. We never saw one of them without the other one.

Preston was tall with dark hair, fair skin and hazel eyes. Roy was slightly shorter with a

dark complexion, dark hair and dark eyes. They had a very good sense of humor. Eventually the

three of us had a good laugh about what happened to Preston and his family along with

everyone else in school.

Preston and Roy dated a variety of girls but neither one of them were really ready for a steady

girlfriend. Roy made that clear to me on our first date. But after some time, no matter how hard

he tried to hide it, I realized he had feelings for me. Everybody in school knew he liked me more than

any other girl he had gone out with. I had mixed feelings about it since I wasn't really looking

for a boyfriend at the time. The girl in my Spanish class was, Mya O'Reilly. She was a year younger

than me and was so smart she was skipped a grade.

Mya was average height and a little stout but well built. Her thick, long, dark-brown

hair was gorgeous. She had big, lovely, green eyes that were covered by eye glasses. As far

as bad taste in fashion goes Mya had me beat. I believe we were destined to become lifelong friends.

She was a loner, too, and never bothered with anybody in school. The other students were leery

of her for some reason. On the day that she first spoke to me it was totally unexpected. Yet, there

was a reason why, out of all of the students in our Senior class, Mya chose to speak to me and one I

would've never guessed.

It happened during our second semester of Spanish after I *misplaced* my text book and

the cassette tape that went with it. I was totally baffled when I couldn't remember how I did that. The

last place I saw them was in my bedroom with the rest of my school books. Mysteriously,

they vanished.

Our Spanish mid-term was approaching and it was imperative that I have those missing materials. Without them I couldn't do any studying. I tried to explain my dilemma to

Mr. Dugins, who was our Spanish teacher. If I thought I would get any sympathy from him I was

sadly mistaken.

"If I were you, Miss Moran," Mr. Dugins told me sternly, "I would do everything

humanly possible to find that text book and that tape." I stood there not knowing what else

to say to him. "This school," he continued, "cannot afford to put out money because of

a student's carelessness. That's one less text book and cassette tape for a student in next

year's Spanish class." He had never been married or had any children I'd heard and I could

understand why. The man had no compassion whatsoever and very little patience.

Marshall Dugins was a short, stout, balding man around the age my Dad would have

been. He was merciless in his teaching methods, especially if he knew you could do well in

his class. He always had a noticeable stain somewhere on his shirt. During class he would

take sips from a cup of liquid he kept on his desk. We assumed it was either coffee or tea that

he was drinking. That is, until we started noticing that he seemed to be a little tipsy in class

sometimes while he was teaching. I was sure that Mr. Dugins had a serious problem that nobody

knew about. There were rumors that he did have a wife and children at one time but they left him.

I didn't know how true that was because it could have been just a rumor. Then again I've heard

it said that *where there is smoke there is fire*. Nobody ever knew if what I heard was the truth

or not.

The school gave a student two weeks to recover or replace lost materials. There was no way my

family could afford to pay $125.00 for another Spanish text book, and $60.00 for another cassette

tape. So I desperately needed to find those materials and quickly. After I was laid out by Mr. Dugins,

and the thought of my family shelling out money that they didn't have I was nearly in tears.

"God, Help me," I thought in a panic. *"What am I going to do?"* It was so unlike me to

be that careless. It was then that an unlikely and unexpected source of *help* came to my rescue.

The same source of help that would aid me in my life many more times after that. No matter how

unconventional it was that help never failed me.

"The same thing happened to me once," said a compassionate female voice behind me. When I

turned around there stood Mya O'Reilly looking into my eyes. She smiled at me sympathetically

as Mr. Dugins rolled his eyes at me and walked away. I didn't feel like smiling back at her so I

didn't.

"Sometimes," began Mya, "you think something is lost but it just gets moved." "What?" I

said looking at her confused. She never talked to anybody so I think I was more surprised

than confused. "Things get moved," she continued still smiling at me. "They're not really

lost. I overheard you and Mr. Dugins talking." I was so dumbounded I didn't know what to say

to her. "I'll tell you what, Zo," said Mya, "when you get home from school today look under your

brother's bed." Then she promptly turned around and walked away from me. As I watched her I

thought she was crazy or just plain weird. I was even more surprised that she knew my name.

I liked Mya from the beginning. I didn't know or cared to know why other students were leery

of her but I would find out. I was never afraid of her. After our first encounter I was drawn to

her like a moth to a flame.

All the way home from school that day I wracked my brain about my dilemma. When I

walked into the house Mama was in the kitchen listening to the radio. We greeted each other

warmly. I didn't know how to tell her about my problem. Then a strange thing happened.

Caron's latest single began playing on the radio. As I listened to her fabulous voice Mya's

words suddenly came to my mind. Up until that time I had completely forgotten what she told me. *"Look under your brother's bed,"* she said. Yet, she never said which brother,

Angel or Dami. The strange thing was that I didn't recall her words until I heard Caron's voice.

I went into our living room and laid my purse and school bag on the sofa. Then I went

upstairs to Dami's bedroom. When I looked there was nothing underneath his bed except some

dirty clothes. I was starting to feel a little bit foolish when it hit me. *"How could Mya know where*

my lost materials are?" I thought. After that I went downstairs to the basement where Angel slept.

I looked underneath his bed and got the shock of my life.

Laying there neatly together were my Spanish text book and the cassette tape. I had no

idea how they got there or how Mya knew they would be there. It looked as if someone had

deliberately put them there as carefully as possible. It was almost as if someone was playing games

with me. I was absolutely sure of one thing. Neither Angel nor Dami had any reason whatsoever to

bother with my school supplies. Also, I recalled what else Mya told me.

"Things get moved," Mya had said. *"They're not really lost."* I shuddered a little as I recalled

the day when the television set kept going off by itself. A chill ran down my spine like it had

that day. It was obvious to me then that *someone* wanted me to know they were around me.

And it was *someone* other than those in my household who was making their presence known.

I never wanted to believe in ghosts but I didn't write them off either. The very thought of them

scared me. Something started tugging at the corners of my mind right then. It was something that

was both fascinating and incredible. Mya *knew* things that other people didn't *know*. They were

things that others couldn't have known unless they were like her. I realized why the other students

in school were so leery of Mya. They were afraid of her. Instead of becoming scared like many others

were I became intrigued.

During dinner that evening I was quieter than usual. I couldn't get Mya off my mind. When usually all I thought about was Caron and seeing her again. Angel, Mama and Dami talked

a blue streak with one another. I was so absorbed in my own thoughts I didn't hear Dami

talking to me.

"Earth to Zobie!" cried Dami looking at me. I looked at him as if coming out of a trance.

"Oh," I said, "did you say something to me?" "Yeah," he replied, "I brought some fashion

magazines home for you to look at." "Why?" I asked him indignantly. "So," he said, "maybe

they'll give you a clue about how girls your age are dressing these days." "Oh, leave her

alone," said Mama smiling. "She'll get the hang of it in her own time." "I know, Mama," replied

Dami. "She just looks so plain and drab all of the time. Zo's a pretty girl with a nice shape.

The guys need to see that."

"Well," said Angel looking at me, "you like the way Caron dresses. Don't you, Zo?" "Yeah,"

I replied smiling, "I do." "Then take a cue from her," he continued. As an after thought

he said, "You know I never noticed it before but you look a lot like Caron." "Yeah," said Dami

seriously, "you sure do." Mama smiled a forced smile. She grew quiet when the

conversation turned to Caron. There was something on her mind again like it was that night when

we first met Caron. I had something on my own mind, too. We had a *'guest'* or maybe two in

our house that nobody knew about.

I planned for my family to meet Mya. I was sure they would be as intrigued with her as I

was. They would also get to see that I wasn't alone as far as bad taste in fashion goes. I had

no idea how much Mya would enthrall all of us with what I called her *'talent'*. Through my

new found friendship with her and her gift I made a startling discovery. Not only was something

supernatural going on in our house, but I was horrified when Mya told me what and *'who'* it

was.

Not long after Mya and I became friends I received a mysterious telephone call. It was a telephone call that I never expected and one I would never forget. I thank God for the friend who was there to help me through the many numinous events that were coming my way.

Chapter Ten

The next day in class I thanked Mya for *helping* me. "Oh," she replied, "it was nothing, Zo."

"But how did you know?" I asked her curiously. "You wouldn't believe me if I told you,"

replied Mya. "Try me," I said looking into her eyes. "I knew you wouldn't be afraid of me," she

began smiling, "so how about having lunch together today, my treat. I'll tell you all about it."

"Sure," I told her, "where?" "There's a Deli down the street from here," said Mya. "We'll get some

sandwiches, sit down on one of the walls by the cafeteria and talk." "Alright," I said. "I'll meet you

on the first floor at lunch time."

Mya and I met for lunch that day like we planned. It was a real treat for me. And, nice to

not have to eat a brown-bag lunch for a change. As we sat down on the wall to eat we began to talk.

"So," I said to Mya, "tell me how you knew where my school supplies were." Mya looked into

my eyes. "I know a lot of things, Zo, as you've already probably guessed," she told me nonchalantly.

"Things about people that nobody else knows." "You mean," I began, "you can *see* things, like

visions." She nodded her head. I became more curious. "Do you *know* anything else about me?" I

asked her.

"There's a strong connection," said Mya, "between you and somebody who's famous. I

can't see what it is yet though." Of course she was talking about Caron. She was the only famous

person I had ever known. "That's so weird, Mya," I replied. "What else can you

see?" "Am I right about the famous person?" she wanted to know. I just stared at her. "You can tell me, Zo," Mya continued. "You already know that I'm right." "I did meet Caron Cato," I told her. "And for some reason I've always felt a closeness to her but I don't understand why."

"Who is that?" asked Mya. I couldn't believe she had never heard of Caron. "She's a famous R & B singer, Mya," I said. "I can't believe you've never heard of her. Don't you listen to the radio?" "No," said Mya, "not really. I'm more into reading books than listening to music or watching television. I've probably heard one or two of her songs. I'm not completely out of touch with things."

"You would have to be living on another planet, Mya," I told her, "not to know about Caron Cato." "How did you meet her?" she wanted to know. I told her about Angel, Mama and me going to Caron's concert and talking to her backstage. "You're going to see her again," Mya said. I was very happy to hear that.

"It won't be for a while," said Mya matter of factly. I listened intently and couldn't wait to hear what else she had to say. Then she became very serious as she spoke to me. "Something is going to happen to you, Zo," said Mya. "It has something to do with Caron and the connection that the two of you have." I was fascinated. "It's strange that I can't see what it is right now but it'll become clear," she continued with concern in her voice. "Whatever it is it's pretty strong."

I would quickly learn something about Mya and her *'gift'*. She was never wrong about anything she told me. I continued to listen eagerly as she talked. "There's a guy in school," said Mya, "who's in love with you, Zo." I experienced somewhat of a let down suddenly because everybody in school knew that Roy liked me. "After school tomorrow," continued Mya, "he's going to ask you to be his steady girlfriend." "What?" I said in disbelief bouncing back to my awe of her ability. I didn't think Roy had the nerve to ask me something like that.

"Oh," Mya said, "by the way, your Dad's brother, Wayne, is coming to visit you and your family soon." I looked at her as if she had suddenly grown two heads. We hadn't heard from Uncle Wayne since my Dad and Devon were murdered. Yet, within the next two weeks everything Mya told me except for me seeing Caron came to pass.

Uncle Wayne surprised my family and I when he showed up for a short visit with us. We were overjoyed to see him and he stayed with us for a whole month. We hadn't realized how much we missed him. His resemblance to my Dad was uncanny. On the Sunday he was to leave us a strange thing happened.

I was coming down the stairs that morning when I overheard Mama and Uncle Wayne talking in the kitchen. A sense of urgency was in their voices. I could only make out some of what they were saying. I came in on the tail end of their conversation.

"It doesn't make sense for this foolishness to keep going on," Uncle Wayne said to my mother. "Well," said Mama, "you know how they feel about me. So I guess in some way it applies to the children, too. I've never let it bother me so it shouldn't bother you either." "It's just not right, Anna," said my uncle, "and you know it. Those children need to know one another. They're brothers and sisters and none of what happened is their fault." When I walked into the room they greeted me cheerfully.

"Hey, Zo," said my uncle smiling. "How are you this morning?" "Fine, Uncle Wayne," I replied smiling back at him. "Would you like to go over to your Uncle Caleb's and Uncle Arnet's houses with me today before I leave?" he asked me. I was surprised. Mama said nothing as I looked at her then at Uncle Wayne. My siblings and I had never been to either one of our uncle's houses that I could remember. We never met any of our cousins either. It was strange since all of us lived in the same town. They could've gone to the same school as my older siblings did and didn't know one another. I agreed with Uncle Wayne. It wasn't fair for my uncle's wives to take their dislike of Mama

out on us. "Sure, Uncle Wayne," I said eagerly.

Although Mama didn't say anything I could tell that she didn't approve. She certainly

didn't look happy about it. "I would take all of you," said Uncle Wayne looking at me, "but you're

the only one at home right now." I wasn't stupid and I did overhear part of his and Mama's

conversation. My uncle wanted to take me to see my other uncle's houses for a reason.

Uncle Wayne said that he just wanted to tell his brothers good-bye. Soon we set out

walking and stopped at Uncle Caleb's house first. Imagine my amazement when I counted only six

blocks from my own house. To say Uncle Caleb was surprised to see me would be an

understatement.

Uncle Caleb's wife, Dana, was at home with him. She was short, plump, brown-skinned

with mixed gray hair and dark eyes. Their children were all grown with families and homes

of their own by then. I looked at the many photographs on display in the house while

the three adults chatted happily with each other in the kitchen.

I saw a wedding photograph of my Dad and a woman I knew had to be Bedelia. They were

young and looked very happy. I noticed Uncle Wayne watching me as I looked at the

photographs that were arranged around the wedding picture. I stared at them then turned to

look at Uncle Wayne. For the first time in my life I knew that I was looking into the faces of my

other siblings when they were children. One picture of a little girl seemed hauntingly familiar to me.

If I hadn't known better I would've believed it was me in the picture. She looked so much like

me but I did know better. I don't know why I never asked the adults there about any of the children.

Uncle Wayne smiled at me.

I stared at the little girl in the picture. She could've been someone else as a child that I was familiar with, too. It was like I was being drawn to the photograph. "Let's go now, Zo," said Uncle Wayne jarring me out of my reverie. By that time he knew I had a chance to see all of the photographs. "My flight leaves at two thirty this afternoon," he told my aunt and uncle, "and I want to stop by Arnet's house." We said our good-byes and left.

My uncle and I took a bus to Uncle Arnet's house which was across town. We were warmly greeted by him and his wife, Zelda Mae. She was medium height, slender, dark complexioned with light-brown eyes and dark brown hair. Aunt Zelda couldn't stopping fussing over me. She and Uncle Arnet were happy to see us.

While the adults talked I looked around. I saw a lot of the same photographs in their house that I saw at Uncle Caleb's. I could tell that Uncle Arnet was very fond of taking pictures. However, there were no photographs anywhere of Mama or of me and my siblings. Suddenly, there it was again. I looked at Uncle Wayne who was watching me. He smiled as he nodded his head to me. It was the same haunting photograph of the little girl that I saw in Uncle Caleb's house.

I started to get the feeling that Uncle Wayne wanted to tell me something but he said nothing. Maybe he was waiting for me to ask questions but I didn't know how to do that at the time. The little girl's picture bothered me. She looked so much like Caron Cato would've looked as a child. Of course I shrugged that off as being ridiculous. Why would any of my family members have a photograph of Caron Cato as a child? I couldn't stop staring at the photograph.

"It's time for us to leave now, Zo," said Uncle Wayne after a while. Aunt Zelda hugged and kissed me asking me to please come back to see them. She was very nice and so was Uncle Arnet. Whatever happened with Mama, my Dad and his first wife was over as far as they were concerned. Before we left Aunt Zelda took a picture of my uncles and I together. Then Uncle Arnet took one of me by myself. "These will go on the mantel with the other pictures," said Uncle Arnet happily.

On our way home I recalled something else that Mya told me. *"Something is going to happen to you, Zo,"* she told me. *"It has something to do with that singer and the connection the two of you have."* I was stunned. *"No,"* I thought, *"that isn't possible."* I tried to dismiss what I was thinking because it was so far fectched. *"It just couldn't be."*

However, a wonderful thing had happened to me. I visited with my family and finally got the chance to see what my other siblings looked like. They were older then so I knew they looked different. Yet, I still got the chance to see them. I couldn't get the photograph of the little girl out of my mind for a long time. I didn't know it then but Mya knew a lot more than she told me. She had her own reasons for holding things back from me. I could never have guessed how powerful her gift truly was. Not until she began to reveal other things to me.

Chapter Eleven

Roy and I started seeing each other on a regular basis. My family liked him right away and so did Mya. In fact, all of them liked him and Preston. He tried to hook Mya up with Preston but they quickly realized that they would be better off as friends.

Not only did Mya and I become best friends but the talk of our school. The other students, especially the girls, made fun of us because of our lack of taste in fashion. They nicknamed us *'the odd couple'* but we ignored them.

Roy never seemed to care how I dressed. He told me that I always looked good to him. I knew it was crap. Yet, I did know that he sincerely liked me for who I was inside not what I looked like on the outside. He was never shy about showing me how much he cared for me. Mya was right again.

Although I knew Roy was in love with me I never felt quite the same way about him, or so I thought at the time. "One day," Mya said to me in class, "I'll tell you something else about you and Roy, Zo." "Why can't you tell me now, Mya?" I asked her. "It can wait," she replied smiling softly.

Whatever it was that Mya knew about me and Roy didn't worry me. She was my friend and if it was something bad she would've told me. Also, it was another thing that I would learn about life. There are times when a true friend will keep something to themselves. Some things are really better off not knowing.

The financial situation in our home continued to improve. Dami was on my case more and

more about the way I dressed. That's when I figured out that I was embarrassing my brother.
When he bought me a nice reddish-orange, crocheted dress with a red, silk lining I knew I was
right about that. The dress was short and clingy, too. I had to admit that I loved it so I thanked him for
it.

After that Dami started buying me more clothes and so did Angel. Then along with Lee they
starred giving me money to buy my own clothes. I had fancy jackets and tee shirts
in various colors that were low cut. With Mya's help I sewed rhinestones onto all of the
jackets. I wanted them to look like the ones that Caron wore.

I was a thrilled to finally have clothes that only *I* had ever worn. Mya took a cue from me and
changed her style of dressing, too. Our new fashion sense was quickly noticed at school. We
got a lot of compliments as well as attention from the girls and the guys. A few girls even began
to copy our style. Never in my life did I think I would be a trend-setter.

There were advantages for me being the youngest child in our family and a girl. Whereas, Mya's
father could always afford to give her an allowance each week. Now the same girls at school who used
to make fun of me and Mya started trying to be our friends. But there were still other girls who would
look at us and just roll their eyes. Experiencing envy and jealousy from other girls was definitely
something new.

Mya and I started getting invitations to house parties and get togethers. One girl went out of her way
to become friendly with us. Her name was, Jolia Scott, and she was one of the most popular girls in
our school.

Jolia was pretty, tall and shapely with dark hair and hazel eyes. She came from a
well-to-do family in a nice area of town. In fact, she lived only a few doors from where Patsie
and her mother used to live and had known them very well. To my surprise, Jolia was a very nice

person and truly down to earth. Yet, no matter how good she treated us Mya never really warmed up to

her. All she ever told me was that something was *off* about Jolia. "I can't put my finger on it yet,"

Mya informed me with a puzzled look on her face.

I learned to trust my friend's instincts. Sometimes people's lives aren't what you

think they are. You just never know about some people. Jolia always had a cheerful smile

for Mya and I. She loved to talk, especially to me, and we were in the same history class.

Nobody would've ever guessed how lonely she really was.

"You know, Zo," Jolia said to me in class one day, "it's eerie how much you look like

that singer, Caron Cato. I never noticed it before. You two could be sisters, especially

the way that you dress now." I wasn't surprised by her remark. Lately I was hearing the

same thing from a lot of people. Mya and I always thanked Jolia and her friends for their

invitations to parties or just to hang out together. But outside of school we never bothered with any

of them.

We finally got a telephone in our house and it was installed in the kitchen. Then some time

later Lee had one installed in Mama's bedroom. I threw a lot of hints around about having one of my

own. It took a while but I finally got one and was ecstatic! It was instrumental to my spending more

and more time alone in the house. However, if I thought my bizarre experiences were over I was

wrong.

I still listened when Mama and Gram Zela talked about the supernatural and spirits.

According to them some people were extremely sensitive to that world. I took everything in that

I overheard as well as about how mysterious God Is. I learned a lot by listening to them. For one

thing, I realized that it wasn't a coincidence that Mya came into my life when she did. And we had

much more in common than we ever knew.

I got to meet Mya's father, Lonnie. Her mother, Eubya, came from Egypt and died from

Leukemia when Mya was twelve years old. I saw pictures of her all over their house. She

was beautiful and Mya told me she had inherited her gift from her mother. She resembled her

a great deal. On some nights her mother would come to her and tell her things. That was spooky.

Mya was the only child her parents had.

I became a regular fixture in Mya's house which was only two blocks away from mine. Her

father was nice. I liked him and he liked me. From the first day Mya set foot in my house she told me

that someone other than Mama, Angel, Dami and me was there. Also, that the *presence* was not a

hostile one. It was someone who loved us and would never harm us. No matter how much Mya tried to

reassure me I got scared anyway. Who wouldn't be scared knowing that somebody you cannot see is in

your house with you watching you all of the time?

One afternoon Mya and I were in my bedroom talking. No one ever knew about the

incident with the television set except Dami. Many other things had happened to me since then

that I could not explain. "Has anything strange ever happened to you in this house, Zo?" Mya

asked me. "Yes," I answered surprised by her question. I began to tell her about the many frightening

things that happened to me.

I would be sitting down somewhere and suddenly see something moving out of the corner of my

eye. I would put something in one place and it would be moved to somewhere else like my

school supplies were. A personal item I put on my bureau dresser was laid on top of my

pillow when I left the room and came back. Sometimes I could feel someone's breath on my ear and

hear whispering. It always unnerved me. Once I made a sandwich, put it on a plate and

sat the plate on the arm of a chair. I left the room to get something. When I came back the

sandwich was sitting on top of the television set.

Another day I put an outfit I was going to wear to school on my bed. After that I

went to the bathroom. When I came back into my bedroom the outfit was neatly folded on top

of my bureau dresser. I was so upset I stayed home from school that day. Mama thought I

was sick when I didn't come downstairs that morning. I broke down and told her what happened to me.

Other things that had happened came spilling out of me, too. Mama tried to comfort me. I was

surprised that she believed me. She always believed me as if she had experienced some strange things

herself in her life. However, she never told me about any of them.

The worst time was when I was laying in bed sound asleep. I was awakened by

someone's hands around my ankles swinging my legs around in the air. I laid there

terrified then screamed hysterically! Mama was home and came running into my bedroom. I guess

she thought I was hurt or something. I didn't want to tell her what really happened so I lied when she

questioned me. I don't know why.

"I-I thought I saw a mouse," I told her shakily. "What?" Mama said dumbfounded. She

put her hand to her chest. "My, Lord, girl," she said, "it sounded like you were being attacked

or hurt." Someone was always bothering me in our house yet I never saw see anybody there.

One evening I was standing at the kitchen sink washing dishes. Someone walked right up

behind me while I was standing there. I felt and heard the impact of each step they took but

when I spun around nobody was there. No one else was in the house at the time.

I was in bed asleep one night when someone knocked on my bedroom door. It was an

eerie, ghostly-sounding knock that awakened me. Somehow I knew no one but me would've

heard that *knocking*. When I opened my eyes I saw my brother, Devon, smiling at me. As I watched

his spirit faded right into my bedroom wall. He was wearing the same clothes he had on when he and

Patsie went to the Dance that night. On more than one occasion I thought I saw my Dad.

I was sitting at our dining room table doing my homework one night. The chair next to mine was pulled away from the table. It was as if someone was getting up from the table or getting ready to sit down. Again I saw no one there. I jumped up, ran upstairs to my bedroom and slammed the door closed behind me. I was trembling as I curled up into a fetal position on my bed, petrified with fear.

"Zo!" I heard what sounded like my mother's voice calling to me from her bedroom. I didn't answer her. I was so scared I couldn't get my lips to move even if I wanted them to. To make matters worse my mother wasn't at home. She couldn't have been the one calling to me. But someone did. "Zo!" I heard my mother's voice again. I started trembling as I prayed silently for God to help me.

I recalled another afternoon when I was watching television in the living room. Someone was slowly coming down the stairs behind where I was sitting. Each step creaked louder as whoever it was got closer to where I was sitting. I stood up, turned around slowly and looked toward the stairs. I saw someone's legs but no other part of their body. Horrified, I ran toward the front door as Angel entered the house. By the look on his face he knew that something was wrong.

"Hey," he said concerned, "what's wrong with you, Zo?" I couldn't speak at first. "You look like you just saw a ghost, girl," he continued as he stared at me. "N-nothing," I told him nervously. I sat down relieved that somebody came home and I wasn't alone in the house anymore. But I realized that I was *never* alone in that house. Also, that I was being targeted.

Faith had carried our family through so much. Mama told us that God was always with us. As long as we kept our hand in His, He would never Allow anything or anyone to harm us. I relaxed as I recalled her words. Gram Zela would tell us the same thing. They said that when things like that happened somebody was trying to tell us something important. Usually it was a warning of some kind. Whoever was bothering me definitely wanted something.

I couldn't imagine what they wanted or what they were trying to tell me. All I could think about was, *"Why me? Why not go to Mama or somebody else in the family?"* I wished I wasn't so scared. Maybe I could have been brave enough to ask them what they wanted. There was something else coming for me and my family. Like before when it did come we would be totally unprepared for it.

Sunday afternoon was when I mopped and waxed the floors in the living room and dining room. One Sunday Mama and Dami decided to go grocery shopping. I started to move all the furniture so I could clean behind it. When the water got too dirty I went into the kitchen to change it. After I changed the water I came back into the room. Every piece of furniture I had moved was put back into its' place. I gasped in horror dropping the bucket of water. I fell to my knees and started sobbing softly. Angel came home from work and found me crouched in a corner of the room staring blankly into space. He put his arms around me gently.

"Hey, Zo," he said softly lifting me from the floor. "What's happening to you, girl? Talk to me." Yet, I couldn't talk to him. I was so upset by then and just wanted to be left alone. Quietly, I went upstairs to my bedroom and laid down on the bed. After that incident more strange things continued to happen. I was almost seventeen years old by then. But had no idea that things would get even worse.

I decided to leave home because I was so tired of being haunted. That way I thought I could get some relief but there was no escaping it. I tried to stay with Gram Zela, Gina and Lee. However, it didn't help because whoever it was followed me. I was always filled with anxiety wondering what would happen to me next.

Before I left her house to go back home Gram Zela came to me. I was sitting on the sofa when I noticed her watching me from her kitchen. She walked over to her sofa and sat down beside

me smiling tenderly.

"Come here, Zo, honey," she said as she hugged me closely. She began to gently stroke

my hair. "You don't have to say anything," Gram Zela said softly, "if you don't want to. But

you should know you don't have to carry this burden alone." I looked at her wide-eyed

because it was obvious that she knew what I had been going through.

"You mean," I said surprised, "you know, Gram Zela?" "Of course I know," she

replied lovingly. "You're just afraid of the unknown, honey. Just remember what we always

told you. It's usually someone who loves you very much and you love them. They would

never harm you." Tears came into my eyes as I looked into hers.

"I just don't know," I sobbed gently, "why they're only bothering me, Gram Zela. Why

me?" My grandmother spoke to me softly. "Didn't your mother ever tell you," she began,

"that you were born with a veil over your face?" I was confused. "No, she didn't" I said. "What's

a veil, Gram?" "Well," said Gram Zela, "in my day children who were born like that could

see and sense things that other people can't." "What is it?" I asked her again. "It's a very

thin layer of film over the baby's face when they're born," she replied. "The midwives

would just wipe it away."

"Mama never told me about that," I said. "I wondered why she always believed me when I

told her things." Gram Zela chuckled softly. "She should have told you about that," she said. "Maybe

you wouldn't be so afraid of the spirits." After my grandmother told me about 'the veil' I didn't feel so

spooked anymore. I even felt better than I had in a long time.

I understood why Mya and I were so close and why she chose to talk to me. In a way I had the

same gift that she did but I never knew it. Although I felt better it didn't stop me from being completely unafraid. It was something I would have to get used to now that I knew about it.

When I told Mya about the 'veil' she knew all about it. Then she told me just what was happening to me. According to her it was my father and my brother, Devon, who were trying to communicate with me. They were doing it for reasons that no one would have guessed. Rather I should say for reasons I would have never guessed. Mya knew all along what my father and brother wanted. She just didn't know how to tell me. I will always love my dear friend for her compassion and understanding. No one could really help me but God so I had to rely on Him. There are things in life that are beyond human help.

"They're the main ones, Zo," Mya told me. "But they're not the only ones who are trying to reach you." I felt a slight panic attack that I know it showed in my face. I thought about the woman who was calling to me that day and knew it wasn't my mother. "Just pray for courage, Zo," continued Mya. Then I had a bright idea. "Maybe," I said, "they can come to you, Mya, and you can tell me what they want." Mya chuckled softly. She knew it was my cowardice talking.

"Okay," said Mya. "If you're willing to try that I'll help you since you're scared." "Alright," I replied quickly, "let's do it and see what happens." I truly thought that it just might work.

"The next time you're home alone," began Mya, "call me on the phone and I'll come right over. We'll see what we can do." I breathed a sigh of relief. "I feel better about this already," I told Mya happily. "I can tell you right now," said Mya, "what I sense about all this." "What?" I asked her curiously.

"Do you remember me telling you," began Mya, "that there's a connection between you and that singer?" "You mean, Caron," I said puzzled. "Yeah," Mya replied nodding her head slowly. "You think all of this has something to do with her, Mya?" I asked. She just looked at me. "But what?" I asked.

"These spirits," said Mya, "are coming to you, Zo, because of something to do with Caron. Your Dad, your brother and a woman are involved." My heart fell. "A woman?" I said confused. *"Maybe it was Patsie I heard that day,"* I thought immediately. The woman sounded like my mother but it could have been Patsie. My Dad, Devon and her died so horribly. Their lives snuffed out in an instant. I was always sure they were still together. It was obvious that their peace was being disrupted for some reason.

Whatever it was they wanted at least now I had someone to help me. I wasn't sure if I would be up for the task but I learned something else. You would be shocked when you're doing the very thing you thought you would never be able to do. Talking face to face with a dead person would be at the top of anybody's list. As my mind wandered Mya looked at me strangely.

"What is it?" I asked Mya. "It wasn't who you think it was, Zo," said Mya. I looked at her confused. "The woman," continued Mya, "you heard calling to you that day from your mother's bedroom. It wasn't who you think it was." I thought she was reading my mind. Mya never failed to amaze me and I would find out that she was right. It wasn't Patsie. When I found out who the woman was I was really stunned.

Chapter Twelve

Another day Mama, Angel and Dami went out and I was left home alone. Remembering our plan I telephoned Mya and asked her to come over. After she arrived we sat down on the sofa in the living room to talk. The music on the radio was playing. It seemed like we waited a long time for something to happen. The telephone rang so I got up and answered it.

"Hello," I said into the receiver. At first there was no response on the other end of the line. "Hello," I said again a little louder. "You're going to be very important, Zo," said the ghostly but familiar voice of a man. "What?" I said confused. "It won't be much longer now," he continued. "Your sister is going to need your help. Just don't be afraid." Suddenly the line went dead. Slowly I hung up the telephone and turned to Mya who was staring at me.

"What is it, Zo?" asked Mya. "S-some man was on the phone," I said still confused. "His voice was eerie." Mya didn't say anything. "He told me," I continued, "that I'm going to be important and that my sister is going to need my help. It was weird, Mya. He said for me not to be afraid." I *was* afraid but Mya remained calm as she looked at me.

"Did his voice sound familiar to you?" Mya asked me quietly. I thought about that for a few seconds as my eyes widened. "As a matter of fact," I said, "his voice was very familiar." A smile came upon Mya's lips as I looked at her curiously.

"What is it, Mya?" I asked her not really wanting to hear her answer. Deep down inside me I already knew who the man on the telephone was. "You have heard his voice before, Zo," replied Mya.

"It was your Dad. His name was, Joe, right?" My stomach fell to my knees. I hadn't heard my father's

voice so long time. And not once did I ever tell Mya what his name was.

All I ever told Mya about my father was that he was murdered along with one of my

brothers and his girlfriend when I was a little girl. No one in my family mentioned my

Dad's, Devon's or Patsie's name to her. I was being haunted by my father and Devon but not Patsie.

"Oh, God, no!" I cried trembling as I sat in a chair. I was go glad Mya was there. I don't know

what I would have done if I had been alone. I shook my head in disbelief. How was I going to

handle the knowledge that I could connect with the realm of the dead? The very thought of it sent chills

down my spine.

"But how is that possible, Mya?" I asked my friend in a soft, frightened voice. "I can't

imagine how I can become that important. What is it that I'm going to do for one of my

sisters that nobody else can do? I just don't understand." Mya was so calm it was scary.

She was used to strange, spooky things going on but I wasn't. As far as I was concerned I never

would be.

"There's something in your family," began Mya, "that you and your siblings don't know yet,

Zo. Your Dad is not talking about Venna or Gina." I looked at her as if she had suddenly

sprouted horns on her forehead. "Don't be surprised," she continued, "every family has

their secrets."

"I don't understand what you're talking abour, Mya," I said. She continued to smile at

me. "Why are you lying to me, Zo?" she asked. "Your Dad had other children besides you

all didn't he?" I looked at her in silence. I wasn't surprised that she knew about my Dad's other

family. And I'll never know why I tried to hide it from her.

"I'm sorry that I never told you about them, Mya," I said. "I know," she replied. "You should know that I can't just *see* things about people, Zo. I can *hear* things, too, that other people can't."

She surely had a fantastic gift. It was obvious that my Dad himself told her about his other

children.

"Nobody in my family has ever really talked about my other siblings," I informed Mya sadly. "I

haven't thought about them in a long time either. We've never known anything about them."

"Someone knows a lot about them, Zo," Mya told me. When she said that the first person who entered

my mind was Mama. "Not knowing one another," said Mya, "is not what your Dad wanted. But it

made somebody else happy that you didn't know them." Again Mama came to my mind. I always

suspected that she was the reason why we never knew our other siblings.

"Zo," said Mya, "your Dad and your brother, Devon, have been trying to tell you about

this other sister for a long time. I could tell you but it would make you more scared

and they don't want that. It's best if you discover things on your own and you will." I

was even more amazed at Mya.

"Can you understand now, Zo?" Mya asked me. "They know you're scared so they've

been trying to get your attention any way that they could. If you knew your other siblings it

would really help." "I wouldn't know where to start, Mya," I replied, "except for my

mother. And I don't think she would be too forthcoming." Mya got up and put her arm

around my shoulders sympathetically. "Your Dad," she began, "was stopped from making that happen,

Zo." I got a little angry when she told me that.

"Don't worry," Mya said compassionately. "Just let things happen like they're supposed to." "I

don't know how to be brave about this like you," I told Mya. "And why could I hear my Dad now and

not before?" "Because," she said, "a medium is here with you. Another link between the living and the

dead like you. Now that they've established contact they won't need to try so hard anymore." I got nervous as I believed I knew where Mya was going in our conversation.

"I don't want to see any ghosts, Mya," I said fearfully looking at her. She chuckled softly.

"Spirits won't show themselves to you if they know you're afraid," replied Mya. I calmed

down. "By the way," she said, "who is Patsie?" My friend couldn't have shocked me more

if she had deliberately tried. I told her about Patsie and how she was the girl who was murdered along

with my Dad and Devon.

I never stopped wondering about the strange telephone call that I got from my Dad. Mya was

steadfast in her decision to let me learn things on my own and in the end it was the best way.

I started wondering about my other siblings again. I wanted to know where they were. I could've

gotten information from Uncle Wayne but after his divorce he vanished. We didn't know where he was.

It was clear when Uncle Wayne took me to visit my other uncles he was trying to tell me

something. I recalled all of the photographs in Uncle Caleb's and Uncle Arnet's houses. Photographs of

him and Bedelia's wedding day and the children's pictures arranged around it. Also, the photograph of

the little girl that I would never forget. My uncle wanted me to question him about the children in the

pictures that day. I couldn't work up the courage to do it. Now I wished I could go back to that day but

I couldn't.

After I received that eerie telephone call there were no more ghostly encounters for a long time. I

even dared to think that the haunting might be over. However, Mya assured me in no uncertain terms

that it wasn't. It wouldn't be over until I helped the sister that I didn't know.

One day Mama, Mya and I were in our kitchen listening to the radio. As we sat at the table talking

Mama tried to sing along with her favorite songs. Then the latest single by Caron came over the air

waves. Mama got quiet.

"She's coming to Milika on her tour," said Mya referring to Caron. Milika was a fairly big town not too far away from Harly. "I think it's next year," continued Mya. "Really?" I said a little excited. "I would love to see Caron again." Mama said nothing. "I was thinking," began Mya, "maybe we can go to that concert since it's not far from here. What do you think, Zo?" I realized what Mya was doing.

"That would be great," I told Mya following her lead. "It's been a long time since we saw Caron hasn't it, Mama?" Mama forced a smile but said nothing. "We had backstage passes," I told Mya as if she didn't already know that, "from Angel's girlfriend at the time. But we don't see Minda like we used to. She's probably pretty busy working for a big Concert Promoter if she's still working for him."

"She is very busy," replied Mya. I don't know why I looked at Mya surprised that she knew that. You would think I'd be used to her 'knowing' things by then. Neither I nor anybody else in my family ever told her anything about Minda either.

"Maybe," suggested Mya, "you can try contacting Minda. And she can get some more passes for this upcoming concert. It would give you and Caron a chance to see each other again. This time you might be able to sit down and talk to each other for a while." A cup Mama had slipped from her hand to the floor and broke into pieces. She nervously got up from the table. Mya and I eyed one another. Our whole dialong had been to see how Mama would react.

"Oh," said Mama, "I-I'm so sorry about that. I don't know what happened. The cup just slipped from my fingers." She started to clean up the mess as Mya and I watched her. The cup had not just "slipped" from her fingers. My mother got nervous when Mya mentioned Caron and I being able to talk to one another. And the way she said it was as if it was something that Caron and I needed to do. Also, something that clearly upset Mama. My mother was full of more secrets than I knew.

As Caron's song continued to play on the radio my entire body started to feel unnaturally chilly. I shivered involuntarily. "What's wrong, Zo?" Mya asked me. "I don't know," I answered her confused. "A chill just came over me out of nowhere." I caught Mama's glance

at me out of the corner of her eye.

The hairs on my forearms and the back of my neck began to stand on end. I shuddered

slightly again. When Caron's song finished playing as suddenly as the chill came

over me it was gone. I was confused. *"What was that about?"* I wondered.

When I looked at Mya she had a crooked, little smile on her lips. A smile that made me

realize that she knew more than I would believe. I nodded my head to her as I smiled

back. I understood. Until I heard Caron's voice on the radio I was alright. But Mya knew

what happened to me. Caron and I were so connected spiritually I could feel and sense how she was

feeling whenever she sang a particular song.

I recalled stories that I heard about identical twins. How they could feel each other no mattered

how far apart they were from each other. It was the obvious closeness that they shared as well as

blood.

After that it didn't matter where I was. Whenever I heard one of Caron's songs a chill came over

me. When the song was over the chill was gone. It was more than a little spooky. When Mya finally

did tell me why that was happening to me I was glad that I never knew. If she had revealed the truth

to me before she did I know I wouldn't have been able to handle it.

First of all I wouldn't have believed it even knowing Mya was genuine and wouldn't lie to me.

Everything that was going on with me had something to do with Caron. She was still waiting for the

special song that she wanted to sing. A song that would show her true depth as a Performer and an

Artist. An etude written only for her. There was a reason why she hadn't gotten it yet. Believe it

or not the problem was largely Caron herself.

Chapter Thirteen

As Mya and I grew closer so did Roy and I. Then a new guy started going to our school in the middle of the school year. Jacob O'Condor was in Mya's Homeroom class. He was tall, dark and handsome but always had a strange look in his beautiful, dark-brown eyes. It was as if he was harboring some deep, dark secret that he couldn't share with anybody. As it turned out he did. Mya never had any interest in the guys at school until Jacob came along. Right from the beginning they had feelings for each other. Once they started dating they were a handsome looking couple, too.

Jacob began to hang out with Roy and Preston. But he didn't have a love for computers like they did. In fact, Jacob hated computers. He thought they caused more problems in the world than did any good. For a teenager Jacob was a bit old-fashioned. The five of us had our own little group and we loved it.

Jacob lived with his parents and two younger sisters, Dinah and Serell. His mother's name was Dinah, too, and she was around my mother's age. Miss Dinah was a nice lady. She was average height with long, brown hair, light-brown eyes and brown skin. Jacob, Sr. was a tall, stout man with a fair complexion, dark, mixed-gray hair and dark-brown eyes.

Jacob told us that his father was fifteen years older than his mother. He looked a lot like his Dad. His sister, Dinah, was fifteen years old and his other sister, Serell, was thirteen years old. Both of them were pretty and resembled their mother.

Jacob, Sr. was a supervisor at the lumber yard and Miss Dinah was a Homemaker. She used to work part time as a Registered Nurse. For reasons that Jacob didn't tell us she had to stop working.

I wondered what would make her quit a good job like that and I wasn't the only one. It wasn't hard to

surmise that the reason must not have been a good one. My family liked Jacob. Although Mama

thought he was kind of brooding for a teenager. I had to agree with her on that.

I thought I had died and gone to heaven when Angel came home with a new stereo. My friends

and I had a good time with it on the weekends. We stayed at my house playing records and learning

new dances. Jacob was like my mother. He loved to sing along with the songs that he liked and he had

a terrific voice. All of us were taken aback the first time that we heard him sing.

"Wow!" we all cried looking at Jacob after we heard him singing. "You should check into a record

deal, man," said Roy. Jacob just smiled. It was one of the few times that he ever smiled. When I heard

him sing I couldn't help recalling the great voice that my father had.

Jacob had his heart set on becoming a Chef because he loved to cook. Which is why he was

enrolled in the Home Economics class in our school. "He'll be a singing Chef," joked Mya

chuckling softly. I could tell she was growing more and more fond of Jake as we started to

call him. It was easy to see that the feeling was mutual whenevver they looked at each other.

One Saturday night we were sitting around my living room. Angel came home and to my surprise

and joy Minda was with him. Most of our family was there and everybody was happy to see her.

Nobody knew that she and Angel had started seeing one another again.

"Where have you been all this time, Minda?" Venna wanted to know. "We haven't seen

you in a long time." "Well," began Minda, "I've been really busy. We have a big tour

coming up soon." "What tour?" asked Gina. "Caron Cato's tour," replied Minda. "That's

right," said Mya. "Remember I told you about that, Zo? She's coming to Milika." "I thought that was

next year," I replied. "Well," said Minda, "it's been moved up to the Fall."

"I heard about it on the radio the other day," Lee chimed in. "Maybe," said Angel looking at Minda, "you can get us some more back stage passes, Min." Minda smiled. "I'll see what I can do," she said. "A lot of people want them. There's only a certain amount that we can give out unless Caron says otherwise."

"At least," continued Angel looking at my friends and I, "try to get some for these five." He would automatically get a stage pass for any concert because of Minda. Purposely I looked at Mama and said, "How about you, Mama? Wouldn't you like to see Caron again?" "That's okay," she said quietly. "You kids go." I thought she might be eager to see Caron again but it was obvious that she wasn't. Minda changed the subject as she looked at me.

"So which one of these handsome young men is yours, Zo?" Minda asked glancing at Roy, Preston and Jake. "Guilty!" cried Roy happily. "And I would love to meet a celebrity like Caron Cato." "So who else belongs to who?" asked Minda looking at Preston. "Don't look at me," he said quickly. "I'm unattached and I like it that way." "Then that leaves you two," said Minda smiling as she looked at Mya and Jake.

"I wouldn't mind meeting somebody famous like that," replied Jake. Mya said nothing. "It's all set then," said Minda. "I'll try to have passes for all of you by the end of next month. Anyway, I have a feeling that when I mention Zo's name to Caron she'll give me all of the passes that I want." I became curious.

"Why do you say that, Minda?" I asked. "Caron has never forgotten any of you, Zo," said Minda, "not you, your Mom or Angel." "Really?" I said feeling flattered. "Out of all the slew of people that she meets she still remembers us?" "I kid you not," replied Minda. "She talks about you at times, Zo. It's as if there's some kind of bond that she feels with you." "Hm-m-m," commented Mama a little suspiciously. "That is strange. Does she ever say *why she feels that way about* Zo ?" "No," said Minda, "not to me anyway. All she has ever said is that she felt a kinship with Zo that she couldn't

explain." Just then a chill ran down my spine and I shuddered. Minda noticed it.

"Are you alright, Zo?" asked Minda curiously. "S-sure," I replied shakily. "I'm fine." "Are you sure,

Zo?" asked Mya looking at me. She was quiet for all of that time before she decided to speak. Then

she looked at Minda and said, "Do you know Caron well, Minda?" "I think so," Minda replied. "I am

privy to a lot of things that are going on with her." As the conversation progressed it seemed like Minda

and Mya had known each other for years instead of only for about an hour. Or maybe it was that

my friend knew something about Minda that the rest of us didn't. "Like what?" prodded Mya.

A forlorn look came upon Minda's face.

Everyone was quiet as all of us looked at Minda waiting for her to answer Mya. I realized

that she asked Minda about Caron for a reason and that reason was most likely me. A soft smile came

on Minda's lips. When she spoke we couldn't help but hear the dismay in her voice.

"That's the thing," began Minda, "when you work closely with some celebrities. You

become aware of what going on in their personal lives that nobody would ever guess. Things that you

really wish you didn't know about." It wasn't hard to see that Minda really cared about Caron. And

there were things going in her life that she was troubled about. She tried her best to stop the tears that

started to well in her eyes. I recalled the horrible argument we overheard between Caron and her

boyfriend that night. Mama broke an awkward silence.

"We don't have to hear about that girl and her private affairs," said my mother nonchalantly.

"Why not?" I asked incredulously. "If Minda wants to talk let her." Mama's problem was that we might

find out more about Caron than she wanted us to. I'll never understand why people hide things.

Sooner or later every secret will surface no matter how long it takes. My mother already knew

that because she found it out the hard way. Mya continued to press Minda for information about

Caron.

"Is the same man still in her life, Minda?" asked Mya. Minda looked sad as she spoke. "Yes," she answered, "unfortunately he is." "Does he still treat her badly?" Mya wanted to know. Everyone looked at Mya in surprise except me. None of them knew about her stunning ability yet.

"Come to think of it," said Mama, "I don't think it's such a good idea for you to bother Caron anymore, Zo." "Why not?" I asked her surprised. I couldn't understand why her feelings toward Caron had changed so much. "Yeah," said Angel curiously, "why not, Mama?" She stumbled for an answer. "I-I just think," replied Mama, "you should leave her alone especially since she's having problems."

"Caron's problems have nothing to do with her and Zo becoming friends, Mama," Lee said to my mother. "Just let her be!" exclaimed Mama becoming upset. We were all surprised by the way she was acting. "In fact," continued Mama, "all of you children should leave Caron Cato alone." My siblings and I looked at one another confused. Something wasn't quite right and they knew it. Mya remained calm and unmoved by my mother's behavior.

In spite of the way Mama was acting Mya continued to question Minda. "Well, Minda," said Mya, "does that man still treat Caron badly or not?" Mama promptly got up and left the room.

"What made you ask that?" Minda asked Mya. Mya was smart. She wasn't ready for Minda or any of the rest of them there to know about her gift. "I've heard some things," continued Mya, "about Caron and him. Things that aren't too cool."

No one but me knew that Mya had already seen the sad situation that Caron was in. I knew everybody began to suspect that Mama was hiding something. A far away look was in Minda's eyes as she started to speak.

"It doesn't matter," said Minda somberly, "how hard you try to make somebody see something. If they don't want to see it they won't. Denial is a terrible thing. You just can't force somebody to see what they don't want to see." "What are you talking about, Minda?" asked Angel. Minda sighed and shook her head. Through Minda Mya opened a doorway that was going to allow us to see into Caron's life. Suddenly a look of anger crossed Minda's face.

"Zane," said Minda nastily, "treats Caron like dirt. I can't stand that bastard. He beats on her whenever he feels like it." "What?" everyone cried at the same time in disbelief. "We didn't see any bruises on her," replied Angel, "on the night that we met her." "He's one of those low lifes," said Minda, "who knows how and where to hit you so the bruises don't show. After all, he can't have Caron canceling shows because she has a black eye or two, right?"

"My, Lord!" cried Venna completely stunned. "Why does she put up with that creep?" "Who knows?" said Minda flatly. "I've been asking myself that question for a long time. I've come to the conclusion that some women really think that's love." "What the hell is wrong with Caron?" asked Angel dumbfounded. "I don't know," replied Minda. "I just don't know."

"There is something wrong with her," said Mya calmly. Everyone looked at her curiously. "Emotional abuse," she continued, "can leave scars on a person's spirit and mind. They are terrible scars that sometimes never heal." All of us kept quiet as we realized Mya had more to tell us. After that she spoke as if she was watching Caron's whole life from a distance.

"You won't believe this," said Mya matter of factly, "but Caron doesn't think she can do any better than him. He's taken her self esteem almost to an all time low. That's because he's so low down himself." "That's crazy," interrupted Angel. "As beautiful and talented as Caron is she doesn't need him. I don't understand it." "You're right about that," agreed Minda. "But she thinks she needs him. If you can wrap your head around that. Nobody would believe the things she lets him do to her."

Caron was five feet five inches tall just like me and slender. Her performances were called 'explosive and exciting' by people in the music industry. She was an unbelievably great singer and dancer and who had millions of fans around the world. Also, she had a lot of fun on stage. From what I saw of Zane Mattox he was around six feet four inches tall. He had dyed blonde, curly, shoulder-length hair, brown skin and hateful-looking, dead-brown eyes. If the eyes are the mirror to our soul like I've heard he was a demon from hell.

Whenever I saw Zane he looked like he was high on something. It could have been either drugs or alcohol or maybe both. He always looked stoned in all of the pictures I saw of him and Caron. The public wasn't fully aware yet of her personal problems as Mya and Minda were. Eventually all of that would change.

When Mya decided to let everyone there know about her gift they were fascinated. I wished Mama was still there. It would have been priceless to see the look on her face. Needless to say, she did find out. The conversation continued and our curiosity was highly peaked by that time.

"Tell us what else you know about Caron, Mya," said Gina. "Sometimes," replied Mya, "she feels like she wants to give up her career." "Why?" asked Venna as surprised as we all were to hear that. "She has never gotten the song she really wants to sing," answered Mya. "Only some singers get the song that will live on long after they're gone. Very few song writers ever know what is truly in a singer's heart and soul."

"You mean," said Minda, "like a special composition just for them." "Exactly," replied Mya. "An etude if you will." "Etude?" said Lee confused. "It's pronounced differently," said Minda, "than it's spelled. There are only five letters, e-t-u-d-e, but it's pronounced 'a-ty-ood.'" "That stumbling block is in her way," said Mya. Everyone grew more enthralled with Mya. Even Minda learned things about Caron that she never knew. The kind of things that the entertainment world would have a 'field' day with.

"You really do have psychic power," exclaimed Roy looking at Mya in amazement. "Wow!"

"I've been able to see things about a person," said Mya, "from the time they are a child until they are old." After she said that even I got a little scared but it passed quickly. I could tell by the looks on all of our faces everyone else got a little fearful, too. Mya chuckled softly.

"Don't worry," said Mya jokingly. "So far I've never been able to tell anybody the day that they're going to die. Some things only God Is supposed to know." However, Mya would see someone's death. And there was absolutely nothing that any of us could do to stop it.

Mya was steadfast where Caron and I were concerned. Yet, she was determined to hold back things and let them happen in their own time. It really didn't matter. I couldn't have done anything about them anyway.

The 'sister' part of my father's message to me was still a mystery. When everything did come together and begin to make sense it was mind-blowing. As we listened Mya began to tell us Caron's life story and we were even more amazed by her. But in private she told me things that she didn't tell the others.

Chapter Fourteen

Caron was twenty five years old. Her real name was Corinne Atocano and her mother's name was, Bedelia. When Mya told us that I immediately recognized the name from somewhere but couldn't recall where. Her mother changed all of her children's last names to her maiden name after she divorced Caron's father. She never wanted to talk to any of them about their father. And readily told people that he ran around on her with another woman for many years. He had other children with his mistress and later married her. Caron was twelve years old. Her father was a tall, dark and handsome man. She inherited her amazing singing voice from him.

We were surprised when Mya informed us that Caron had not been in touch with her siblings for years. Although she and her siblings had deeply loved their father her siblings sided with their mother and greatly resented him. Being the youngest child didn't stop Caron from witnessing his treatment of her mother just as the others had.

Eventually Caron's mother met another man and fell in love with him. Unfortunately, he was married and living at home with his wife and children. Ellis Maxwell and his wife, Bina, had three teenage sons. Caron's mother believed Ellis was going to leave Bina to be with her. For three years he kept putting Bedelia off with one excuse after another. When she finally realized he wasn't leaving his wife it enraged her.

A terrible fight broke out between Caron's mother and Bina. Bina's family got involved in it the matter, too. As Mya told us about Caron's life it was like watching a movie unfold before us. You could hear a pin drop in the room.

At this time Bina's youngest brother was known as one of the worst trouble makers in town. On the night of the fight between the two women he gave Bina a loaded gun. She shot Caron's mother first then shot Ellis who died immediately. Bedelia hung on in the hospital for two days suffering from a gun shot wound to her stomach before she died. Bina went to prison receiving only fifteen years for both murders. However, she only served six years. While in prison she was diagnosed with having advanced breast cancer and died a year later after they released her. The brother who supplied the gun got nothing but was killed in a bar fight soon after Bina went to jail.

I saw God's justice in that situation. Two people would have still been alive if a gun had not been in the equation. Anyone who commits a double homicide should stay in jail for life. But Bina's family had a good friend who was a criminal attorney. He made Ellis and Bedelia look like two people who deserved what they got. Like they were the guilty parties and Bina was just an innocent victim. In my opinion she still had a choice whether to gun somebody down in cold blood or not. I guessed that the jury saw it as I did but still had sympathy for her predicament.

After Caron's mother was murdered she and her siblings went their separate ways. They didn't know that their father had been murdered years before their mother was. Bedelia knew about his murder but managed to keep it from her children. It was easy since none of them cared about him except Caron. She was devastated when her mother's brother told her about her father's murder at her mother's funeral. Our hearts went out to Caron. It was no wonder she looked so sad. There was so much on her mind that she never talked about to anyone but wanted to.

When Caron's parents parted ways she went to live with her maternal grandmother, Suze. She wasn't comfortable anymore living in the same house with her mother and her siblings.

All they talked about was what a terrible man their father was. Suze wasn't like that and she loved and understood what Caron was going through.

Suze recognized Caron's talent as a gifted singer. She entered her into a talent contest when she was sixteen years old just for the fun of it. A Talent Scout from the West Coast happened to be there. Caron won the contest hands down but was too young to be signed to a contract with anybody.

Suze wanted Caron to continue her education. She would never have allowed her to quit school. Unfortunately, a twenty six year old leech named, Zane Mattox, was at the same talent show, too. Unknown to Suze he stalked Caron for the next two years and became involved with her.

When Suze found out about Zane she filed many complaints and even a Restraining Order against him. The guy was bad news from the beginning. He was determined to get keep grubby hands on Caron. After a while she wouldn't listen to Suze anymore.

Before she turned eighteen Caron ran away with Zane to the West Coast. He tracked down the same Talent Scout who was at the contest a years earlier. The man remembered Caron. Still, he contacted Suze and found out that she was still in school and too young to be signed to a recording contract. In the end none of that mattered. There will always be greedy people who cannot see past the dollar sign.

It didn't take Zane long to get a firm grip on Caron's life. He changed her name to Caron Cato yet something must have scared her. While Zane and this Scout were putting things into motion for Caron to sign a recording contract she went back home to Suze. After that she went back to school.

We were captivated by the things that Mya was tellling us. I think that if the house had caught on fire right then none of us would have budged. There was nothing that we wanted to hear but the sound of Mya's voice as she continued talking.

Naturally, Zane followed Caron home. Suze, armed with the Restraining Order that was still in force, forbid him from having any contact with Caron. She threatened him on numerous occasions with jail time. The only problem with that was getting Caron to press charges against him. Suze knew what Zane was from the beginning. No matter what she did to keep them apart Caron wouldn't listen to reason. She would always find a way to be with Zane.

Zane had a lengthy prison record to no one's surprise. From the age of sixteen years old he was a known thief and he used hard core drugs. He was released from prison not long before he saw Caron at that talent show and had served time for selling drugs, guns and Grand Larceny. He had never been married but had five children with four different women. Women who never got a penny from him for child support. The guy never had anything until Caron was signed to a lucrative recording contract months after she finished high school.

Caron started making big money real fast. Zane had never seen that kind of money legally. Immediately he appointed himself as her Manager. He got fifteen percent of everything Caron earned. She never wanted him to be her Manager but she didn't do or say anything to oppose it. She was well aware of his reputation as a thief and his blatant drug use. She didn't like the crowd he associated with either. On top of all that she found out that he was an unscrupulous womanizer.

According to Mya, Caron had a hard time standing up to Zane. It wasn't that she was afraid of him. It was largely because she was in love with him and she thought he loved her. Yet, Mya revealed to us that he told Caron on more than one occasion that he didn't love her but he cared for her. Even I knew that was a lie. Zane was the kind of guy who loved only one person, himself. All Caron ever was or ever would be to him was a meal ticket and nothing more.

She was just another woman he could use. In the beginning Caron didn't care. However, over

the years that changed as did her feelings for Zane. As Mya talked we started to feel

sorry for Caron.

On top of his fifteen percent Zane had been stealing money from Caron for years. He wined and

dined his lady friends as well as the members of the crowd he hung around with. A few of the women

he snuck around with behind Caron's back were members of her own entourage.

One woman in particular was named, Lumell Nicks. She was a little older than Caron was and

was hired to be her Public Relations Manager. She was tall, shapely, brown-skinned and with

Zane whenever Caron turned her back. Lumell started out as Caron's friend. As Mya talked

about this woman the hairs on my forearms stood on end and a cold chill crept down my spine.

Lumell and Zane had absolutely no regard for Caron's feelings. They didn't give a damn if

she knew about them or not. Their affair was the cause of many quarrels between Caron and

Zane. Other than the arguments they had over his stealing from her and his drug use. He

refused to let Caron fire Lumell which was incredulous to us. After all, they worked for Caron

right? Caron didn't work for them.

I wanted to cry for Caron and I felt tears welling in my eyes. As I looked around me at the

others I could see that they were feeling the same way. Mya hesitated as each one of us began to

ponder all that she was telling us. My sister broke an awful silence.

"My, Lord," said Venna softly. "Why would Caron keep putting up with that? I don't

care if she thinks she's in love with him or not. It's obvious he doesn't give a damn about

her. He even told her that to her face. I just don't get it." "I guess," replied Minda, "she doesn't think

that she can do any better which is hard to believe. I know there are probably plenty of guys

out here who would love to be with Caron." Angel looked at Minda and said, "Where is her grandmother now, Min?"

"Her grandmother," said Minda sadly, "is dead now. She was in her late sixties when she had a bad stroke." Minda hesitated. "Caron looks a lot like her, too." She shook her head. "I knew things were bad between her and Zane," she continued, "but I didn't know how bad." "Do you know this Lumell person?" Mya asked Minda. "Yeah," said Minda with a touch of anger in her voice. "I know her. It broke Caron's heart when she suddenly turned on her, too. They were friends which is why Caron hired her in the first place."

Something else became obvious to all of us there. Minda knew a lot more about Caron's troubles than she let on. We noticed all along that she wasn't as stunned as the rest of us were by the things Mya was telling us. Yet, Mya was far from finished with Caron's story.

"As you already said," began Minda, "Caron has been looking for a certain kind of song to sing. There have been a few of them sent to her by song writers. But she never likes any of them." Minda hesitated. "I think Zane has a lot to do with that, too, somehow. There is also a lot of them that Caron doesn't get to see." What was happening to Caron didn't make sense to us. Especially since she had no real use for Zane whatsoever.

Maybe it was because he was the first and only boyfriend she ever had. Caron just didn't know how a woman should be treated by a man even if he wasn't in love with her. Mya began to tell us more about Zane.

Zane Mattox was raised in an orphanage. It was the same one where he was left on the front door steps as an infant. Growing up as a child he was labeled "unadoptable" by the people who ran the orphanage. He was always creating problems there and tried to burn the place down twice. When he was sixteen years old he ran away after being molested by one of the attendants who worked there.

The streets became Zane's home until he went to jail. He sold drugs and ended up becoming

his own best customer which only worked for so long. He started stealing to support his growing

habit. He went from picking people's pockets to breaking into stores then into people's homes.

He lived off various women whenever he could. His way of life lasted a long time before he

was caught and carted off to prison.

Of the four women he had children with he battered three of them. The one that he didn't beat on

tried to take his head off with a baseball bat when he hit her. So he knew not to try that with her again.

Those other three women ended up in the hospital more than once. He was never arrested because they

refused to press charges against him. All they really wanted was to be rid of him and through

Restraining Orders they got their wish. He never bothered them again or even tried to see his children.

Suze's death sent Caron into a severe state of depression for a while. She carried a lot of

guilt, blaming herself for what happened to her grandmother. She was already feeling badly about

her father. Caron couldn't seem to let go of him. He always called her "baby girl". It was strange when

I recalled that my Dad used to call me the same thing.

"Sometimes," said Minda, "I'll catch Caron in her dressing room sobbing softly. If I ask her

what's wrong she always says 'nothing' and smiles. She'll be holding a photograph that she keeps

with her. I asked her once whose picture it is and she told me that it was her Dad. I guess if I asked to

see the picture she would show me but I've never asked. I don't know why." Minda hesitated again as

all eyes were on her.

"It's odd," continued Minda, "but I just remembered something else." She seemed surprised at

herself. "Well," asked Angel anxiously," what is it?" "Caron told me," said Minda, "that she has

dreams of her Dad. In the dreams he is always with a young guy that she doesn't know

but this young guy knows her. Her Dad speaks in the dreams but the other guy just smiles at her and never says anything. She said that she knows it means something but doesn't know what."

"If she mentions those dreams again," said Mya, "tell her to ask the young guy who he is and what his name is." "Alright," said Minda. "I'll remember to do that. Do you think that's important, Mya?" "Yes," replied Mya. "It will answer some questions for Caron. She is carrying a lot of heartache. That's why her father and this young guy keep coming to her in her dreams. There is something that they want her to know."

"Wait a minute," cried Minda as if she had another revelation. "Caron told me that she dreamed of her mother once and the same young guy in the dreams with her Dad was with her mother. All he did was smile at her but neither him nor her mother said anything in the dream." "That's weird," said Gina. "Those dreams have to mean something. I wonder who that guy is." Mya looked at me and smiled slily.

"You're right," said Mya. "Just tell Caron to ask the guy his name, Minda. Don't forget that." Minda looked at Mya strangely. She knew as we all did that Mya knew something that she wasn't telling us. Then Mya looked at me again with a 'knowing' smile on her lips. Caron's dreams didn't only mean something for her but for me, too. Not only would questions be answered for her but for me as well. Suddenly out of nowhere brother, Devon, suddenly crossed my mind.

Chapter Fifteen

According to everything that Mya told us Lumell Nicks was a dangerous woman as far as Caron was concerned. As she continued to talk to us about Caron I felt scared for her. "She's definitely worth watching," said Mya, "but she won't be the cause of Caron's down fall." "What does that mean, Mya?" I asked. "Someone else is far more dangerous to Caron than either Zane or Lumell. A person who is in love with Caron but they know she would never have them." "Who?" all of us asked her at once. "I'm not sure yet," replied Mya looking away from us. I knew she was lying.

"I just can't believe Caron's letting people treat her like that," said Dami shaking his head in disbelief. "It's unreal," replied Minda. "You should see the expensive cars, clothes and jewelry that Zane and Lumell buy for themselves." We looked at Mya. She suddenly seemed to drift away from us as if she was in deep thought.

"Are you alright, Mya?" Venna asked her. Mya looked at us with tears in her eyes as she spoke. "Someone is plotting to murder Caron," she replied softly. We were shocked. "What?" everyone cried in unison. "Murder?!" "You can really see something like that, Mya?" asked Jake in amazement. A crooked, little smile came upon her lips as she looked at Jake. I got the strange feeling that he was afraid that Mya may see something about him that he was hiding. I didn't know how right I was about what I was thinking.

"After everything I just told you," Mya calmly said to Jake, "you doubt me?" Jake shook his head. "I-I'm just stunned that's all," he nervously replied, "t-that you can see so much about a person."

"Sometimes," said Mya, "things get muddled but it all becomes clear after a while." We could tell that there was something on Jake's mind.

"What's wrong, Jake?" asked Roy chuckling a little. "Is there something about you that we should know?" Jake eyed him strangely but said nothing. Nobody could have missed the look of panic that was in Jake's eyes, although he tried his best to hide it. "No," he replied quickly trying to shrug it off, "o-of course not."

"How long have you had your gift, Mya?" Angel asked curiously. "As far back as I can remember," answered Mya. "My grandmother told me I was born with it and my mother had it. My grandmother had it, too. She taught me not to be afraid of it and to use it to help people if I could." "You can probably help Caron," said Gina anxiously. "Sorry," said Mya with a half smile. "In her case she's going to have to help herself. If she doesn't nobody else will. And, if she didn't listen to Suze about Zane she won't listen to anybody else. No matter what their abilities are."

"What about the plot to kill her?" asked Dami. "Surely you could warn her about that, Mya." "Caron probably wouldn't believe her," Minda chimed in. "There is a good chance of that," replied Mya. "A dangerous person is surely around Caron but it's not Lumell. I just can't see who this other person is. I can't see what their role is in Caron's life yet. There aren't many people Zane allows to get close to her. He's trying to isolate her more and more but that's hard to do with a celebrity. So it has to be someone who has already been around Caron for a long time. In fact, they've almost as long as Zane has. And don't forget what else I said. Whoever it is they're in love with Caron. They are obsessed with her."

It was strange that Mya *couldn't* see who the person was who was so dangerous to Caron. However, Dangerous enough to want her dead. She always said that some things only God Is meant to know and she was right. Still, I knew that she wasn't being totally truthful with us. I believed that Mya knew who the killer was. When I look back to that day I understand why she had tears in her eyes when she

revealed that there was a murder plot against Caron.

"There is another man coming into Caron's life soon," continued Mya breaking into my thoughts.

"Really?" replied Minda surprised. "Who is he?" "He is a Musician," said Mya. "He's been around her

but he's very unassuming so she has never paid attention to him." "That fits," said Angel. "It's the only

way that Zane and Lumell wouldn't consider him a threat." "Right," agreed Minda, "since they

treat Caron like a prisoner." "It's through this man," continued Mya, "that Caron will gain more

strength." "Good," said Lee happily, "she'll have a chance to get away from Zane, Lumell and

that crazy person who wants to kill her whoever it is."

"Not so fast," said Mya. "When all of them find out about this new man they will know that

they're all in trouble. Undoubtedly, Caron will be getting rid of them but it will be too late. She will

already be talking to other Musicians, Agents, Promoters and Managers. And, she's going to get the

kind of song she wants to sing." We were happy to hear that.

It was hard for any of us to believe that somebody wanted to kill Caron because of unrequieted

love. We heard about things like that happening every day. But until it is someone close to you it

doesn't affect you personally. It was just the way of the world. Our own family members were

murdered under circumstances like that. When what Mya told us came to pass I had never felt that kind

of devastation, not even when my Dad and Devon were killed. Maybe I never felt it so badly because

I was a young child when it happened to them. I wasn't a child anymore but a young woman.

Silently I prayed for Caron's safety as Mya continued to surprise us.

"The Musician that I see," began Mya, "is somehow connected to Caron's murder." All of us

became wide-eyed with shock. "No," continued Mya noticing the look on our faces, "he's not involved

in it. I just don't know how." We were speechless as we stared at Mya. She stopped talking while we took in everything she told us. "I-is there anything more," asked Gina breaking the silence, "that you want to tell us, Mya?" Mya cleared her throat then began to speak again.

"For a while," continued Mya, "it will all be a mystery." Then she added something else that gave all of us chills. "Caron's spirit is going to be instrumental in bringing her killer to justice." We looked at Mya as if she had lost her mind. She had finally came right out and was telling us that Caron wouldn't indeed be murdered. Also, that her soul was not going to be at peace.

"I know what you're all thinking," said Mya. It was Lee who asked her the question that we had on our minds. "Are we talking ghosts here, Mya?" he asked her softly. Mya half smiled. "Until her murder is solved," she replied, "no, her spirit is not going to rest. And, the only way it will be solved will be because of her." I caught the strange look that was on Minda's face. I wish I had paid more attention to it but I didn't. Cops have a hard time catching some killers because they look in the wrong direction.

Mya told us more about the Musician who was coming into Caron's life. He was dealing with his own personal problems of course. A major problem that no one around him knew about except one person. The person who was in love with and obsessed with Caron. Mya told us that she couldn't see what that problem was. I never did believe her about that.

I learned another valuable life lesson. You never know somebody as well as you think you do. People can always surprise you in either a good or bad way no matter how long you have known them. The bad way is always worst than you could imagine. Mya went further and told us that it was after this Musician helped Caron she would be murdered. Right then it seemed so long ago when Mama, Angel and I met Caron.

I wouldn't find out until further down the road that Angel always had the same feeling about Caron that I did. She always felt like part of us. Her story as Mya told it to us was tragic and frightening. I had an overwhelming desire to see her face to face again.

When Caron was scheduled to come to Milika, Mya and I would be out of school. We planned to find jobs right away. College wasn't in the picture for either one of us although Mya could have gone if she wanted to. Our minds were made up. Back stage passes or not we were going to Caron's concert. It didn't matter if anybody else in our group or in my family was going or not. I couldn't wait to see her again.

Chapter Sixteen

It was the last semester of our senior year in school for me and my friends. Mya and Jake were almost inseparable. Roy and I grew closer as well. Yet, none of us, including Mya, had any warning of the horrible tragedy that was shortly to interrupt our young lives.

All Mya and I talked about was Caron's upcoming concert. We followed her tour around the world in magazines and newspapers. Her picture graced the front covers of all of them. Angel was excited about it, too. And, before long Mya, Roy, Jake and I were preparing for our high school graduation. Not one of us was interested in going to the Senior Prom. We just wanted our diplomas.

The night of our graduation ceremony was warm and beautiful. Before getting dressed I stood outside on our front porch. It seemed like there were a million stars lighting up the sky. It felt strange that I never bothered to notice them before. After I got dressed I sat down in the chair by my bedroom window and my mind drifted.

A wave of sudden sadness washed over me as I recalled the night that Devon and Patsie went to the Dance. It was a memory still fresh and vivid in my mind. The night was just like that one and they were so happy and excited. Someone knocked on my bedroom door lightly and jarred me from my reverie.

"Come in," I said softly. Mama entered the room smiling. I smiled back as she walked over to me and hugged me tightly.

"I'm so proud of you, Zo," said my mother sitting down on my bed. "If only your father was here to see our baby graduate from high school. So many years have passed." I could see the tears welling in her eyes. Although she was happy she was also sad. "It's okay, Mama," I told her. "I have a feeling he and Devon are here. I'm glad Zuroi and Aziel came home on leave to see me graduate. Aren't you?" "Yes," replied Mama, "I am but you know they won't be around long."

Neither one of my oldest brothers ever said anything because they didn't have to. But everyone in our family knew that they couldn't stay in that house for very long. They had been that way since my father and Devon died. For that matter they didn't want to be in Harly at all anymore. Years later when Angel confided in us our suspicions about that were confirmed.

"Everything in this house," Angel told us, "and in Harly reminds them about what happened that night. They just can't stand it although they love all of us very much." We understood how they felt. As seldom as it was we were always happy whenever Zuroi and Aziel did visit with us. Until they both decided to get married that's how it was. They brought their wives home to meet us and stayed around for a while. Then Zuroi moved to Germany and Aziel went to live in London. After that the only way we heard from them is through the letters they wrote. And, once in a while we got a long distance telephone call.

Mya's father was at the graduation ceremony and took tons of photographs of us. He was so happy as was everyone else. "Oh," he said as he hugged Mya tenderly, "my baby girl is on her way now." There was that 'baby girl' again. I felt a moment of sorrow when my Dad's face appeared in my mind. As I stood alone someone gently tapped me on my shoulder.

I turned around to see who it was but everyone was off talking to other people. Nobody was there but me and nobody could have moved away from me that fast. I couldn't see

anybody but *someone* was standing there with me. I got a little shaky as I walked over to where the rest

of my family were standing.

Four years earlier our graduating class consisted of six hundred students. On that

graduation night only two hundred fifty of us were there to receive our diplomas.

Unfortunately, all of the others had dropped out and some were dead. One of those who

died was Jolia.

Two months before our graduation Jolia ran off and got married. Her parents were not

happy about what she did but they didn't make a big deal out of it. She didn't have to get

married but it was what she and her new husband wanted to do. We heard rumors around

school that Jolia's Dad had been molesting her for years and she just wanted to get away

from home.

The last time I saw Jolia she was overjoyed to be traveling down South to pay her

new husband a visit. He was a soldier stationed at a military base down there. Everyone

could see how happy she was and how in love she was. A week before graduation she

was scheduled to return home but she never made it. On the way to see her husband the

train she was on derailed and crashed. There were no survivors.

Nearly three weeks before, instead of celebrating our graduation together, I stood looking down on

Jolia at her funeral. One thing I would never forget was her infectious laughter. Her husband, Rodney,

accepted her diploma as well as her award for being our class Valedictorian. He choked back his tears

during the speech she had written until he couldn't continue with it.

Not long after graduation Jake started to complain about having bad headaches. The pain killers

that he took didn't seem to help him. Mya, Roy, Preston and I suggested that he see a doctor and he promised that he would. When we didn't see him for a few days we decided to stop by his house. When we saw Jake our hearts fell because he looked so terrible.

Jake had dark circles under his eyes like he hadn't slept in days. Even a small patch of his hair had turned white since we last saw him. He looked frail like he hadn't been eating. He didn't look anything like the person we knew. The worry on his parent's faces was clear to us. We didn't stay long because he made it obvious that he really didn't want any company not even Mya.

Then Mya started having strange, eery dreams that were more like visions. "I keep seeing the same thing, Zo," she told me, "every time I close my eyes to sleep." It was easy to see that they were unnerving her. She was saddened by the dreams and there would be tears in her eyes when she talked about them. No matter what she said I could tell there was something that she wasn't telling me. As time went on she became more and more upset.

"I can't seem to shake these visions, Zo," Mya said to me one evening while we were at my house. "They have to mean something, Mya," I told her trying to sound compassionate. "I know," she replied. "Why else would I keep dreaming that I'm at a funeral? Jolia is in the dreams sometimes smiling at me." I was stunned. "Jolia?!" I cried. "Mya, you never said anything about Jolia being in the dreams." "I didn't want to scare you," she said. "I don't know if it's a man's or a woman's funeral and Jolia never says anything in the dreams. But she's always standing next to the coffin." "Maybe," I replied, "it's someone close to her." Mya shook her head in confusion.

"I hear a man singing at the funeral," continued Mya sadly, "but I can't see him. He has a beautiful voice that I know I've heard before. I just can't remember where or who it was." "Try not to worry too much about it," I told her with empathy. "Sooner or later you'll remember. Whoever he is I have a feeling that's whose funeral it is." Mya nodded her head

sadly. I had no idea how prophetic my words would prove to be.

It was on a Saturday morning two weeks later when my family and I got that horrible

telephone call. Jake's mother went into his bedroom that morning and found him dead.

Everyone who knew Jake was devastated. We were shocked when later that same day we

got the news that Jolia's husband, Rodney, committed suicide. He never did return to his

military base after taking a leave of absence.

Rodney had started taking anti-depressants. He couldn't get himself together after Jolia's

tragic death. He used his service revolver to put a bullet into his head. My friends came over

to my house later on that day. We talked about both tragedies but mainly about Jake.

"Last night," began Mya solemnly, "I dreamed that Jake and I were in my kitchen cooking.

He was singing. It was the same song I'd been hearing in those dreams I had about the

funeral." "That's whose funeral you saw, Mya," I replied.

Roy and Preston had no idea what we were talking about. Yet, all of us recalled how much

Jake wanted to be a Chef and how beautifully he sang. His death was a mystery to us. He was

nineteen years old. Besides the bad headaches he never complained about having any health problems.

Three months would go by before Jake's parents revealed that he had a terrible drug

problem. He had been using heroin for years and it was slowly killing him. It was only a matter

of time before he got a bad batch of the stuff. His parents thought he had stopped using drugs.

Especially after his release from the last rehab center but he started up again.

They thought moving to Harly would help by getting Jake out of a bad environment. All

it really did was help him get better at hiding his habit. No one ever saw any signs like tracks

on his arms. We were amazed to learn about the places on the body where addicts can shoot heroin. Unbelievable places that nobody would even think of.

Jake had been getting high on the same batch of bad drugs for weeks. That's why he was suffering from the headaches. His body was slowly shutting down. During the autopsy the Coroner saw that all of his inner organs had exploded. What a horrible death.

None of us would have ever guessed that Jake was a drug addict. Our dear friend died from a drug overdose that was inevitable. I'll be wondering forever how his problem got past Mya never mind the rest of us. Then again I figured maybe she didn't *want* to see it.

Jake's funeral was held inside his home. His family did things like they did in the old days. He was laid out in his coffin in their living room. I wasn't surprised at how hard his body looked. He looked like a fifty year old man instead of a nineteen year old boy. It looked like everyone in Harly came to his funeral and there wasn't a dry eye in the house. Minda stood next to Mya and I.

"I'm so sorry, girls," said Minda sadly. "I really liked Jake. I think he was a nice guy who got swallowed up by this world is all." "I can't understand it," replied Mya tearfully. "I can't understand why I never saw it. I can see anything about other people but I never saw Jake's problem. Why is that?" Minda hugged her. Mya hugged her back then walked away from us to be by herself. I couldn't understand it either. She and I were close and she could see things about me. It was just like I thought. She didn't *want* to see anything bad about Jake.

Minda and I went to my house. As we sat around the living room with my family we talked about the funeral. Then Angel abruptly changed the subject as he turned to me.

"On a lighter note, Zo," said Angel, "did you and Mya ever get those back stage passes to Caron's concert from Minda?" We had completely forgotten about Caron's upcoming show. "No," I replied, "not yet." Minda looked at me and smiled. "I'll take care of it," she said.

Caron's concerts were always sold out. Rumors were going around that scalpers were charging people $1,000.00 for a ticket. It sounded a bit exaggerated to me but you never know. If there was a singer worth paying $1,000.00 to see in person it surely was Caron Cato. But that was just my opinion and I was biased.

Chapter Seventeen

That summer Roy decided that he wanted to spend part some time in the South. He had

family there that he hadn't seen in a long time. I had an eerie feeling I would never see him again.

Everyone understood he had to get away after Jake died. The two of them had grown so close

and Roy was still carrying the pain of his loss. It was a warm, sunny afternoon when I stood in the

doorway of the bus depot and waved goodbye to my sweetheart.

Mya and I got hired at the local Post Office. Our jobs were not hard and the pay was good.

Preston went to stay with his relatives in the East. After that he was off to college in the Fall. I didn't

know it then but we would never see or hear from him again either.

Preston always had the same pain in his eyes that Roy did after Jake's death. It wasn't easy

to watch my friends walk out of my life. Although Mya never said anything I could tell she was

feeling the same way as me. In her own way she was still recovering from Jake's terrible loss,

too.

From my job I started to save a little money and help my mother. After so many years

of poverty our family was doing well financially. We didn't have to watch every penny anymore.

It was fun for Mya and I to go shopping when we got paid. Designer clothing caught our eye

quickly even lthough we couldn't really afford it. It was nice to be able to buy my own clothes with

my own money. We put money aside for weeks just to buy some designer jeans with matching

tops. We liked the conservative but classy look complete with stiletto heels.

"You'll have to wear these heels all the time," the sales lady told me and Mya, "in order to get used to them." She was nice, friendly and not much older than we were. When she walked away from us to help another customer Mya whispered to me, "There's no way I'll be wearing these high heels all the time." I nodded my head in agreement with her.

I always loved Caron's style so it was no surprise to my family or Mya that I tried to dress like she did. Caron wasn't a flashy dresser. Even her stage costumes weren't flashy like most of the female singers I saw. She was more of a sexy dresser but with class. All she ever wore were high heeled shoes. I never forgot how she was dressed when I met her. I stayed with that fashion style and it was a drastic change for me. My family members liked the 'new' me. They made that clear when they saw me one night before Mya and I went out.

"Wow, Zo!" cried Dami grinning from ear to ear, "you look real good." "You know," said Lee, "you look just like Caron Cato, Zo." "Yeah," replied Angel, "you two could pass for sisters." Mama smiled but said nothing. "Well, Mama," I said to her. "Well what?" she replied flatly. "Do you think Caron and I look like sisters?" I asked her. I'll never forget the look on her face. It was a look like she wanted to tell me something but decided not to. "You look nice, honey," she replied nonchalantly.

I watched my mother as she turned and walked away from me. I was still confused why she had changed so much toward Caron. Caron didn't only resemble me but all of my siblings.

My sisters had children by this time. Venna's son, Barney, was two years old. Gina had a little girl, Anna Marie, who was three years old and named after Mama. Both of them had children but neither one of them wanted to get married. I think they had flash backs of our parents' early days together. The children's fathers were prominent in their lives.

I started to realize I had been wrong about something. My sisters and I looked more like my Dad than we did Mama. I always thought it was the other way around but it wasn't. I wondered if my Dad's other children looked so much like him. I would've figured out something for myself a long time ago if I had just bothered to pay more attention.

My sisters and I were dark and pretty with great shapely bodies. I had my pick of any guy that I wanted. But for a long time to come Roy would have my heart. I didn't realize that I really loved him until after he was gone. I had been lying to myself all along. He was my first love so I guess it's true that you never forget that one.

At the time Mya wasn't interested in getting involved with another guy which was understandable. We spent a lot of time together. It didn't take long for ugly rumors about us to start flying around town.

We were rarely seen with guys and you know how people are. They thought Mya's grieving period should have been over.

It's amazing how quickly people begin to judge other people. They come to their own imbecilic conclusions that are always wrong. How do they know what's in a person's heart? We laughed at how ludicrous people can be. And, we knew a lot of it stemmed from jealousy.

The rumors began with other young women like us. Probably because Mya and I were something the guys in our town weren't used to. We were true ladies and carried ourselves as such with dignity and respect. If a guy wasn't respectful to us and our families he didn't have to worry about us anymore. We made that crystal clear.

Mama always said that all women were queens and they should be treated that way. In my opinion she was wrong. Some women didn't deserve to be treated like queens. I wondered if some of them could even spell the word 'lady'. It was a four letter word that wasn't in their vocabulary. However, they knew all of the other four letter words usually used by sailors on a drunken binge. In their early days my Dad certainly didn't treat Mama or Bedelia like queens or with any respect.

If a guy managed to last a few weeks with me and Mya we considered it an honor for *them*. We were never arrogant or acted like we were better than they were. The poor fellows could never figure out what happened when we ditched them. They did nothing wrong. But how do you tell someone that you're just not interested in them anymore without hurting their feelings? All Mya and I wanted to do was have a good time. There was never any sex involved. We were always up front with them about that.

Caron's situation was getting worse. Zane's abuse was getting blatant as well as open. The tabloids started to get wind of their problems. While on tour Caron suddenly collapsed on stage at one of her concerts. It was all over the news. She was in the middle of singing a song when it happened. According to the newspapers she was simply suffering from exhaustion. Yet, through Mya my family and I knew better. The media mentioned Caron experiencing bouts of depression. Like Mya said, trying to open eyes that were already wide open was futile.

I became more afraid for Caron. She was worth millions, not only for herself, but for the music industry. Nobody could convince me that she didn't know she could do without Zane and Lumell.

Rosco, Minda's boss, had been trying his best to get Caron away from Zane for years. It was long before Lumell came along. Then we started reading about a tall, dark and handsome song writer who was new on the music scene.

Baron Bonds was nicknamed the "hitman". Every song he wrote made it to the number one spot on the music charts. He wasn't really new to the music world. It was just that he was finally being noticed. He wanted to work with Caron badly and had been around her but she didn't know him. It wasn't long before the two of them met and Caron was thrilled. It was hot news all over the entertainment world and I was happy for Caron.

Minda told us that plans were in motion for a collaboration between Baron and Caron. Of course once Zane and Lumell entered the mix Caron's joy wouldn't last long. They tried to create all kinds of problems for Caron. It was like they were deliberately trying to sabotage her career. Rosco and others in the industry were planning things that would greatly boost Baron's career as well as Caron's.

Inspite of the confusion that Zane and Lumell were causing Caron and Baron signed a contract to work together. The "hitman" was already in the process of writing the kind of song for Caron that she wanted. The etude Mya told us about. The singer and the song writer worked together on every single detail of that song. Minda knew about everything going on and she kept us informed.

"I'm glad," said Angel, "Caron's starting to get away from that Zane guy." "Yeah," added Lee. "I'd just like to catch him in a dark alley one night." "I'm with you, bro," added Angel. "We could leave him right there," continued Lee, "and nobody would ever know who did it." I was taken aback as I looked at them. They were talking about cold blooded murder. Surprisingly, I was the only one who was shocked. Everybody else was calm and cool.

Over the years a lot of people had offered to help Caron get rid of Zane. Like my brothers they wanted to take him out of the picture for good. It was Caron who stopped them. Nobody had to tell her how foolish she was because she already knew. As Mya told us she had to help herself. That is, if she really wanted to.

While we were talking the doorbell rang so Angel went to answer it. To our surprise it was Rosco. He was looking for Minda. A few minutes later the doorbell rang again. This time

I went to answer it and it was Mya. She had a grave look on her face.

"What's wrong, Mya?" I asked as she entered my house. "Are you busy, Zo?" she asked as she looked at me. "No," I replied, "not really. We were just sitting around talking. Minda's boss, Rosco, is here." "Were you talking about Caron?" she wanted to know. "As a matter of fact," I said, "yes."

I lead Mya into the room where everyone was. Rosco was talking to everyone about Zane. There was a lot of anger in his voice. He hated Zane. There was no doubt about that. Mya and I sat down.

"I wish to God," Rosco continued angrily, "I'd had that son of a bitch knocked off." None of us were surprised by his statement and he knew it. I think everybody there felt the same way about Zane that he did. "Him and that no account bitch, Lumell," he said. "Easy, Ros," said Minda calmly. Rosco shook his head sadly. "It doesn't matter," he said. "I've got a feeling Baron's going to change a lot of things."

"What do you mean by that?" asked Minda curiously. "I see the way him and Caron look at each other," replied Rosco. "Oh?" said Minda. "There's something there," answered Rosco smiling slyly. "I've seen plenty of looks like that between a man and a woman." "It doesn't have to mean anything," said Minda. "Oh yeah," replied Rosco. "There's definitely something happening between those two."

I didn't want my mind to play tricks on me as I noticed the look of disappointment on Minda's face. That couldn't be the case since she didn't like Zane either. Yet, I knew I wasn't imagining things. When I look back I'll never understand how none of us ever saw what was going on. When I say 'none of us' that didn't include Mya. When Mama came into the room I felt compelled to speak.

"I can't wait to see Caron again," I said anxiously on purpose. I saw my mother flinch as if a cold

chill came over her suddenly. It was just the reaction I was hoping for. As I looked into her eyes Mama

knew that I knew she was hiding something. I didn't know Mya was watching me and caught onto

what I was doing.

"Secrets always do have a way of coming to the light," said Mya smiling at me. Strangely,

the title of the new song Baron wrote for Caron was called "Secrets". It was a song about the deep

and emotional pain in her life. A pain that she could never shake no matter how hard she tried.

Caron would never forget the terrible fights her parents had over his Mistress. She remembered how

angry and embittered against him that her mother became. Caron knew how much her father loved her

inspite of the rest of her family. Also, she did try to find him and learn about his other children.

Fueled by hatred her mother made sure she cut off all of Caron and her siblings' ties to

their father. She went out of her way to disconnect them from him completely.

What always hurt Caron the most was that he was dead and buried when she learned about his murder.

Caron deeply resented her family because of her losing her father. I believe she was still

punishing them and herself for what happened to him. She blamed them, especially her mother, for his

dying in such a tragic way. I heard that children tend to blame themselves in situations

like that although it isn't their fault. Her story was so eerily familiar to ours. My siblings and

I lost our father to a senseless murder. We had a tragic and terrible bond with Caron that we would

never have guessed was much deeper than we knew.

Rosco kept shaking his head as he talked about Caron. "That girl would be so much

better off," he said, "if she would just get rid of him." "Don't worry," replied Mya

nonchalantly. "Caron will be free." "Sure," said Rosco, "when she's dead." Minda quickly

and quietly got up and left the room. She went outside to the front porch. Mama followed her. We knew something was wrong as we listened to them talking.

"Minda, honey," said Mama, "what's the matter?" It sounded like Minda was crying but

we couldn't be sure. "I'll be alright, Mrs. Moran," she replied sadly. "I just need a few

minutes if you don't mind." "Sure, honey," said Mama.

My mother came back into the room where we were. She had a concerned look on her

face when she looked at Angel. "Do you know of anything that's bothering Minda, son?" she

asked him cautiously. "No, Mama," answered Angel quickly. They stared into each other's eyes.

My brother was lying and Mama knew it.

"You can tell, too," said Rosco looking at Mama. "I knew I wasn't going crazy." The rest of

us were confused. Something was going on with Minda that nobody knew about. Nobody but

Angel that is. When I looked at Mya she smiled at me but it was a sad smile. We went to my

bedroom after everyone else left. As we sat down on my bed I began to question Mya.

"What's going on with Minda?" I asked Mya. "She's been in trouble for a long time," answered

Mya. "Trouble nobody would ever guess." "Does Angel know?" I asked her. "He suspects

something," said Mya. "Now your mother does, too. She's smarter than you all think she

is. Are you sure she's not psychic?" I pursed my lips. "I'm not joking, Zo," said Mya

seriously.

"Well," I said, "what are we missing here, Mya? Come on, tell me." "Minda is in love, Zo," she

said. "I know that," I replied. "Yes," said Mya, "you all think you know but you don't." "What's

that supposed to mean?" I asked confused. "Even Angel has guessed that," continued Mya, "and that

it's not with him." I was dumbfounded.

"What?" I cried. "Who is it then?" Mya didn't answer me. "Can you tell me who she's in

love with or not?" I asked Mya again. "I can," she replied, "but I'm not going to." "Why not?" I said becoming upset. "I don't want to be the one to tell you," replied Mya, "and I'll ask that you please respect that."

The day would come when we learned why Minda got so upset that night. All of us would learn more valuable lessons not to be forgotten. No matter how well you think you know a person they can always surprise you. Angel and Minda were friends and nothing more. We were totally surprised when we found out who Minda was in love with. She had been in love with this person from the day they met. However, that person was not or ever would be in love with her and she knew it. Ironically, Angel was very close to the object of Minda's terrible affection.

There were many times that I wished Mama hadn't been so closed mouth. It wouldn't have done any good for us to ask her why she questioned Angel like she did. Why we never pulled him aside to ask questions I don't know but we didn't. In the end all my brother ever really had was suspicion not facts about Minda's dilemma. So I guess he was telling Mama the truth after all. Yet, she knew that something was going on.

Chapter Eighteen

Mya, my family and me met, the "Hitman", Baron Bonds who was a real gentleman,

very polite and soft spoken. All of us could easily tell that he was the kind of person who was above

anything petty and nonsensical. He told us that he was six feet five inches tall. He had short, black,

wavy hair and piercing, green eyes. His skin was dark and clear except for a thin, light mustache.

Baron was twenty eight years old and had never been married. Though he informed us that

his first love was music he was very happy when he talked about Caron.

"I like Corinne a lot," Baron began a little somberly, "but I don't know how we'll be able to

work in peace. That boyfriend of hers and his *protege* are trouble that neither one of us need or want."

We knew Lumell was the *'protege'* that he was referring to.

"Somebody else working against us, too," continued Baron a little puzzled, "and it's

somebody just as sleazy as they are. I have a sneaky suspicion that it's another woman."

"Why do you say that?" I asked curiously. "Because I can't see anybody," he continued,

"other than a jealous woman who would try to come between me and Caron."

After that he told us something we didn't know. Something Minda hadn't mentioned to us.

"There was a heated argument the other night back stage," said Baron, "and a lot of

people overheard it. I wasn't there." "Between Caron and Zane?" I asked him not surprised.

Baron looked at me wide-eyed. "No," he said flatly. "Caron wasn't there either. It was between

Zane and Lumell. From what I hear she caught him with another woman. Can you believe that? Since it's no secret anymore about our contract together everybody knows Caron is giving

them both *the boot* soon."

"My, Lord," said Gina, "where was Caron?" "I don't know," replied Baron, "but she was

nowhere around. I hear that Zane and Lumell are always at each other's throats lately. So the

rumors about them being gone soon must be true." "It sounds to me," said Angel, "like Zane

might be moving on to another woman." "Yeah," said Baron, "I wouldn't doubt it. But for

some reason, whoever she is, I don't think she's the other culprit I'm suspecting. It's someone

closer."

"I'm sure," said Minda forlornly, "Caron is not as in the dark as you think she is, Baron.

Quite a few people around her make sure she knows what's going on. Not that it does any good."

What Minda didn't tell us was that she was one of those people. In fact, we found out she was the

main source of information to Caron about Zane and Lumell and always had been. She sounded so

bitter to me. As I listened to her I thought she might be capable of hurting Zane, Lumell or

anybody else who threatened Caron. *"No,"* I thought, *"she's not a violent person like that."*

I tried not to second-guess myself where people are concerned. But all through human history

quiet people committed crimes of passion as they were called. People who had never been in any

kind of trouble in their lives and people you would never suspect of hurting anybody. Some of them

had been well liked and even loved.

"Corinne is a real nice lady," continued Baron breaking into my thoughts. He never referred

to Caron by her stage name. The name that Zane gave her. It felt strange listening to him. It

was as if he was talking about a different person I didn't know. To him that's who Caron

was, Corinne Atocano, the woman not Caron Caton, the Entertainer.

"Maybe," said Gina looking at Baron, "if Zane is out of the way you and Caron can hook up,

Baron." "I definitely wouldn't say *no* to that," replied Baron smiling softly. "You can't ever just assume things," Minda chimed in. "Maybe Caron's fed up with these men." "What's that got to do with real love?" asked Angel looking at Minda. "It sounds like Baron and her are already headed in that direction like Rosco said. Remember?" "Don't be so sure," said Minda almost spat in anger. Everybody was more than a little surprised by her attitude as well as her remark. It was unlike her to sound so snotty and sarcastic.

Baron wrote his first song when he was in high school. A few years later that song was recorded and became a hit. After that he heard one of Caron's songs on the radio. "I knew then," he told us happily, "I had to meet her and work with her one day." At a fund raiser he was introduced to Roscoe who, after hearing some of Baron's work, arranged for him to meet with Caron. On an old piano that Mama had Baron played and sang some of the song he collaborated on with Caron.

The song was about a woman who was devastated by tragedy and lost love. She believed she would never be loved again as she once was. She couldn't seem to find the happiness that she was so desperately searching for. It was like she was in love with a dream. Something she didn't believe was real anymore. The song was perfect for Caron.

Zane may have been part of the reason for Caron's sadness but he certainly wasn't the biggest part. I sensed that yearning inside Caron. Some of us can leave the past behind us and keep moving on. Then again some people just can't seem put that one foot in front of the other one so they remain stuck. I didn't want to believe that was true about Caron but it could be. I was glad she had a great career that wouldn't allow her to be "stuck" in the past.

Our little gathering that night ended on a high note. Everybody went their own separate way. It was late so Mya called her Dad to let him know she was staying at my

house. That same night Mya started *'seeing'* a strange woman around her. It was a fairly young woman

around my mother's age. Neither one of us had any idea who she could be.

Mya told me that she saw the woman everywhere. Fortunately for me I never *saw* her.

However, I did start to sense a 'presence' around me all the time. It didn't take much for

me to know it had to be the same woman that Mya was *seeing*.

Mya told me that she was awakened from her sleep one night. This strange woman was

sitting on the side of her bed looking down at her smiling. "She scared the hell out of me, Zo," Mya

said. "Then she just disappeared into thin air." We couldn't understand why she

was *seeing* this spirit or why I was sensing her presence.

"The next time she comes," said Mya, "I'm going to ask her who she is and what she

wants." "Good idea," I replied. "Then you can let me know what's going on. Can you

describe her more to me?" "You may not believe this," began Mya, "but she looks a lot

like Caron. It's obvious that she was young when she died, too." As things turned out I learned

who the mysterious ghost was before Mya did.

One afternoon I was home alone. While I was in the bathroom I heard somebody come

into our house. After that I heard them walking up the stairs. I opened the bathroom door

slightly to get a peek at whoever it was when suddenly the footsteps stopped. I opened

the bathroom door wider but saw no one on the stairs. When I walked to the top of the

staircase I froze in horror.

Standing nearly at the bottom of the staircase looking up at me smiling was a strange woman

I didn't know. She stared into my eyes but said nothing. Then I realized I *had* seen her

somewhere before but I couldn't remember where. She was dressed in regular clothing and was very pretty. At first I thought she had wandered into the wrong house. Then I remembered

that the front door was locked.

I realized I was looking at the woman that Mya had been *seeing*. The same

woman whose presence I was feeling around me all the time. I wasn't afraid as I mustered

courage I never knew I had.

"C-can I-I help you, Miss?" I asked her nervously. She didn't answer me as she kept

smiling. I was trembling all over. "A-are y-you looking for somebody?" I asked her. "I

think y-you have the wrong house." She began to walk up the stairs toward me. I stood against the

wall terrified as she continued to climb the stairs, walk past me and into Mama's bedroom.

Nervous and trembling I followed her.

"W-who are you?" I asked the woman as I entered the room. She stood in the middle of the

bedroom floor facing me. "W-who a-are y-you?" I asked her again. "W-what d-do you want?"

She smiled at me as she spoke.

"I wanted you to know how much your sister means to me, Zobie," the woman said to me.

"M-my s-sister?" I said shakily. The woman nodded her head to me. "She knows about you

and the others but you don't know about her." I thought she was talking in riddles. "I-I'm s-sorry?"

I whispered nervously. "It was a terrible mistake to take her away from her father," continued the

woman. "I realized that too late. But I'm going to make it up to her. We'll all be together

again. Your brother, Devon, and his girlfriend are with us, too." She chuckled a little.

In horror I knew then who she was. I stood there frozen to the floor. A moment later she confirmed

what I had already surmised.

"My name is, Bedelia," the woman told me. "Tell your mother I forgave her and Joe long ago.

I moved on with my life but not in the right direction. It's time that we all had peace. We have to help your sister first, Zo. Oh, tell your friend that I never meant to scare her." Then she was gone.

"Oh my God!" I cried running from the bedroom. I ran down the stairs, out of the front door and right into Angel's arms. I was still trembling all over.

"Hey, what's wrong, Zo?" asked Angel as he held me in his arms. I couldn't stop shaking. "Tell me what's going on, sis. You're shaking. What happened?" Angel took me inside the house. As we sat down on the sofa in the living room I began to calm down.

"B-Bedelia was here, Angel," I told my brother. He stared wide-eted art me as I told him about the eerie visitation I had. All of us knew who *Bedelia* was.

"My, God, Zo," replied Angel in disbelief, "you actually talked to her?" I shakily nodded my head. He put his arms around my shoulders and held me. I started to sob softly as I listened to him talking. "Caron is our sister, Zo," he said into my ear softly. "She knows who we are but we never knew who she was. It's a damn shame that somebody dead had to come back and tell us." I didn't tell him that our father had already tried to tell me.

I detected anger in my brother's voice. And I didn't have to guess who it was directed at. When Mama came home we told her what happened. To say she was shocked would be an understatement. If Angel hadn't been standing next to her I think she would've fallen to the floor.

Mama quietly sat down in a chair. She looked pale and dazed. We saw tears in her eyes as she slowly shook her head. I couldn't understand why people would put themselves through so much pain when they didn't have to. It was so easy to do the right thing in life instead of the wrong thing.

Mama asked Angel to get the family together that evening. She had some things that she wanted to tell us. I watched her get up and head up the stairs as my brother made the necessary phone calls. I decided that Mya might as well be there, too. I called her and

asked her to come over. Also, I told her what happened to me and who the strange woman

was that she was seeing. She wasn't surprised.

Around seven o'clock that evening my siblings and I gathered in the living room to

hear what Mama had to say. Mya was there, too. It was very quiet in the room as my mother

calmly began to tell us the story of her, my father and Bedelia. We thought we already

knew everything. As it turned out we didn't know as much as we thought. Bedelia's

maiden name was, Atocano, Mama informed us. She confirmed that the woman I saw was

indeed Caron's mother and my Dad's first wife. All of the photographs I saw in my

uncle's houses came to mind. I remembered where I had seen Bedelia. It was her photograph.

"I never gave a second thought," began Mama choking back tears, "about the pain I was

causing someone. He was her husband and those children's father. As for me, being young and

thinking that I knew everything was stupid and selfish. I had no right to do what I did."

"You didn't do it all by yourself, Mama," said Gina referring to our Dad. "That's right,"

agreed Lee angrily.

"It doesn't matter," said Mama softly. "It was still wrong and we can't go back and undo

the hurt we've caused someone." She smiled so pitifully. For the first time I felt sorry for my

mother. She was right. She was a stupid young girl who made a stupid mistake and one that

hurt a lot of people. What made Mama feel so badly was that Bedelia had forgiven her and my

Dad before she was murdered.

"The way she talked to you, Zo," began my mother speaking about Bedelia's spirit,

"I suspect her and your Dad are together now. It is what she always wanted you know." "Yeah,

Mama," replied Lee, "but what does that have to do with *all* of them being together again?" "Yeah," said Venna, "as if something is going to happen to Caron."

"I wonder how they're going to make it up to her like she told Zo," said Angel curiously.

"Is that why you suddenly changed toward Caron, Mama?" I wanted to know. Mama smiled

softly. "I knew who Caron was when we met her that night," she said. "Especially after

she told us about her father and what happened to him. All of you children resemble one

another. Your father had some powerful genes." She chuckled softly.

I recalled the telephone call I got that day from my Dad. He told me that my sister was

going to need me. It was obvious that he was talking about Caron. Yet, I had no idea how

she would need me or how I would be able to help her.

None of that mattered to me. Anything I could do for Caron I would do in a heart beat. We

were still puzzled by Bedelia saying they would all be together again. We tried hard not to

think the worst but how could we not? Something terrible was going to happen. And it was

something that no one could have stopped.

Chapter Nineteen

One night two weeks later an unusually violent storm awakened me. I smelled the rain as it came pouring down and I heard the rumblings of thunder in the distance. It was odd that I saw no lightning because I always thought that one accompanied the other. It was two thirty five in the morning when I looked at the clock on my nightstand.

The house was quiet because everybody else was asleep. I knew I wouldn't be able to go back to sleep. *"Our back porch is enclosed,"* I thought, *"and it's warm outside. Maybe I'll just sit out there for a while."* I got out of bed, put on my robe and headed for the stairs. When I got to the top of the staircase I turned on the downstairs lights. That enabled me to see the downstairs area of the house and the front door clearly. As I was going down the stairs I stopped dead in my tracks. I could see two people sitting on our living room sofa but only their legs. *"I guess I'm not the only one who was awakened by the storm after all,"* I thought surprised.

As I continued going down the stairs I was anxious to see who the two people were who were sitting on the sofa. At least I would have somebody to talk to. My heart began to pound in my chest when I saw who the two people were. I wanted to scream and run but I couldn't move or make a sound. It was my brother, Devon, and Patsie was with him.

I knew they could see the terror that must have shown in my face. Both of them smiled at me lovingly as they got up and walked over to stand in front of me. Devon and Patsie were wearing the same clothes they had on on that fateful night when they and my Dad were

murdered. They looked as real as any human being would look yet I knew they were ghosts.

"Don't be afraid, Zo," Devon's spirit said to me tenderly. "We just wanted to talk to you,"

added Patsie's spirit. "We've been waiting to do this for so long, Zo." Although I could see

and feel their love for me I was still paralyzed with fear. "Now you know," continued Devon,

"that Caron is our sister." All I could do was stare at them.

"Although she knows who you all are, too," replied Patsie's spirit, "she never knew how to tell

you. When you see her again she has some photographs to show you." "That should clear up

any and all doubts," said Devon. Suddenly the look on their faces turned grave.

"Some things are meant to be, Zo," continued Devon's spirit. "There's nothing anybody

can do to stop them you know. Caron's been looking for peace for a long time and it's now

within her grasp." "Unfortunately," said Patsie, "there are people around us sometimes that

never have any peace. They don't want to see anybody else with it either." I was confused

but managed to calm down by then enough to speak.

"W-what a-are y-you talking about?" I asked Devon and Patsie as my body trembled all

over. "You can't make somebody want you," replied Patsie. "You know that, Zo. The person

who's in love with Caron doesn't understand that." "They are dangerous, Zo," added Devon. "But

like I said, some things can't be stopped. The important thing is that we all know the truth."

"You can help Caron in that way, Zo," said Patsie."W-what?" I said. "By making sure that

everyone will know the truth," said Devon. "Mya will help you so this person doesn't get

away with what she's plotting to do." "W-who?" I wanted to know anxiously. "Who is this

person?" "Zo?" I heard Mama call from upstairs. "Is that you? Who are you talking to, honey?"

I watched Mama descend the stairs and come into the room all alone. She couldn't see Devon and

Patsie. As she walked over to me I watched the two spirits out of the corner of my eye smiling at her.

"I heard you talking, Zo," said Mama puzzled looking around. "Who were you talking to?" "Oh, no one, Mama," I replied. "I was unable to sleep that's all. I'm going back to bed now." "Yeah," she said, "me, too. I just thought I heard voices." My mother went back up the stairs. Devon and Patsie stood next to me watching her.

"I wanted you and your family to know something else, Zo," said Patsie. "What is it?" I asked curiously. "Hallie is dead now," she continued. "Last week he got into a fight with another inmate at the institution where they put him. He was stabbed to death." I was stunned. It wasn't so much that Hallie Juxon was killed but the fact that I hadn't even thought about him in years. "It's like my mother always said," continued Patsie. "What goes around comes around sooner or later." "We haven't run into him," added Devon, "so evidently he went in the other direction. I can't say I'm surprised." Of course he was talking about hell.

I never saw the two spirits leave. Suddenly I was all alone standing in the middle of our staircase. I went back to my bedroom and got into bed. I don't know what time it was when I fell asleep again. Movement in the room awakened me that morning. Mama was opening the shades on my windows. The sun was shining brightly. She looked at me and smiled as I sat up in my bed.

"Good afternoon, honey," said Mama cheerfully. "You must've been pretty tired. It's after one o'clock in the afternoon." "That thunderstorm woke me up," I told her still half asleep. Mama looked at me with a big question mark on her face. "You were dreaming, honey," she said. "There wasn't any storm last night." "What?" I said confused.

"Zo," replied Mama, "that would've been great. All we've been hearing about on the news lately is how badly we need rain." I looked at my mother as if she had lost her mind.

"Mama," I said becoming fully awake, "the rain was pouring down. I remember thinking it was

strange to hear thunder but not see any lightning. It was two thirty five this morning because

I looked at my clock. You were awake, too, Mama. Don't you remember coming downstairs and

talking to me?"

"Are you alright, Zo?" she asked me softly with concern in her voice. I just stared into her

eyes as she smiled at me compassionately. "There was no thunderstorm, sweetie," said my

mother, "and you didn't talk to me downstairs." "It woke me up, Mama," I insisted, "and you

were downstairs with me. I could smell the rain."

"Zobie," began Mama, "I do believe you, honey. Maybe you ought to take it easy today."

She put her hand to my forehead thinking I might have a fever. I gently pushed her hand

away. "Mama," I said becoming a little disturbed, "I'm not sick and I'm not crazy either."

"I know that, honey," she replied softly.

"What's going on?" asked Dami as he was walking past my bedroom. I guess he could

hear how upset I was so he came into the room. "Mama thinks that I'm losing it or I'm sick in

the head," I told my brother. He looked at Mama puzzled. "What?" he said. "Zo thinks we

had a torrential thunderstorm in the wee hours of this morning," Mama told him."And I

smelled the rain!" I cried looking from one of them to the other. "No way," said Dami. "No

way what?" said Angel coming into my room. Mama and Dami brought him up to speed

about what we were talking about. All three of them looked at me. I could see the love

for me in their eyes as well as the compassion that was there, too.

"Zo," said Angel, "you know there's a drought. Listen, I'll show you." He turned on my

portable radio to the weather station. As we listened the Announcer was talking about how there had been no rain for the past three weeks in our area. I was stunned but couldn't deny that I must have dreamed the whole thing about Devon, Patsie and my mother.

"So," said Dami looking at me, "it was you, huh." "What?" I said confused. "I didn't know who did it," he continued, "but somebody left the lights downstairs on all night. It was you who left them on, Zo." I wasn't sure if I had turned the lights off or not. But if they were on that meant I hadn't been dreaming. It was real. "After they left," I replied in a whisper, "I must've left the lights on." Mama, Angel and Dami looked at one another then at me.

"What are you talking about, hon?" Mama asked me. "After who left?" "It wasn't a dream," I said. "I know it wasn't a dream now. They were really here. You came downstairs because you said you heard voices, Mama. You asked me who I was talking to but I didn't tell you."

"Hm-m," said Mama thoughtfully. "That's odd. Who were you talking to, honey? You said *after they left*." "It was Devon and Patsie," I told her. "There's no way I was dreaming if the lights were still on and that whole thing really happened." "I guess you're right," agreed Angel. "It had be to real." Mama put her hand to her chest.

"My, Lord," said my mother, "first Bedelia now Devon and Patsie. What in the world is going on around here?" "What did they want, Zo?" asked Angel. "They confirmed that Caron is our sister and that someone very dangerous is in love with her. It's as if, if this obsessed person can't have Caron then nobody else will."

"My, God," said Dami, "one of those nut jobs." "Did they tell you who this person is, Zo?" asked Angel. "No," I replied, "but I think they kneow. They just didn't tell me. Devon said that some things can't be stopped." "It's not meant," said Mama, "for us to know some things." "He kept saying that," I said. "What?" said Dami. "Devon," I replied. "Some things are meant to be." Everyone was quiet as we thought about what happened to me. I wondered why my mother was in the vision.

"Oh," I said breaking the silence, "Patsie said that Hallie Juxon is dead. He was killed in the asylum last week by another inmate." "I can't say I'm surprised," said Mama. "I'm surprised that it didn't happen a long time ago," said Dami. Nobody was really concerned about Hallie or even cared. We had forgiven him a long time ago for what he did to our family. We couldn't live or find any joy in our lives if we held onto hatred and unforgiveness in our hearts.

We talked in my bedroom for a little while longer. Then we heard voices downstairs as someone entered the house. The voices were muffled at first.

"Hey, is anybody here?" It was Minda. "We'll be right down, sweetie," Mama called downstairs to her. She had a sly smile on her lips as she looked at us. "Alright," answered Minda. "We'll be in the living room." Mama, Angel and Dami left my bedroom and headed downstairs. "Oh, my God!" I heard Dami cry in excitement. I was curious why he sounded so thrilled.

We often had visitors but no one really special. I got out of bed and hurried downstairs. There, sitting in our living room, was Caron Cato herself. After her talk with us, my mother went to visit Rosco and asked him to arrange for Minda to bring Caron to our house to meet us. However, she never told him the reason for her request. They didn't think anyone noticed but Rosco had a thing for my mother. He would do anything for her. We knew she liked him a lot, too. I realized that was the reason for Mama being part of my vision. If she had not done what she did it was highly probable that my siblings, Caron and I would never have had a chance to get to know each other. Immediately I telephoned Mya so she could meet Caron, too.

There were lots of kisses, hugs and tears. Of course Caron came to our house disguised like nobody would ever believe. There was no way anyone would have guessed who she was. That disguise was peeled away layer by layer right down to her heart. We loved each other although we were not raised with Caron or any of the others. Also, she confirmed that she knew all about us because our Dad told her long ago. He even showed her photographs that he had of us. I was surprised. We promised ourselves that we would never let Caron get away from us again. Such is the human heart we truly meant to keep that promise. I had completely forgotten what I was told by the dead. All of us were so happy together. Caron stayed at our house until a week before her show in Milika was to happen. Every night we enjoyed each other's company and tried to make up for a lot of lost time, as if that was possible. Sometimes it was just Caron and I alone.

It was wonderful when she showed us pictures of our Dad. Caron had a lot of photographs of him that we had never seen before. All of the pictures were taken by Uncle Arnet. I even saw the same photograph of Caron as a little girl that I'd seen and wondered about in his and Uncle Caleb's houses that day. Even Mama enjoyed looking at a lot of my Dad's old photographs, and Caron gave us many of them to keep.

We grew to be extremely close to each other. I was closer to Caron than I was to any of my other siblings. We loved each other so much. The night she left our home for Milika was very sad for us, especially for me. I comforted myself with the thought of seeing her again soon at the concert and thereafter.

Spending so much time alone with Caron did me good. I wasn't afraid of being alone anymore. My sister being a celebrity boosted my confidence tremendously but not to the point where I was arrogant. It did the same thing for all of us although so far no one knew about Caron being our sister except Mya. It was a lot of fun for us keeping a secret like that, too. Caron wanted the world to know and was anxious to tell everybody. But the rest of us thought it would be better to announce it at the concert in Milika.

The whole family was going to be there. It was going to be one of the biggest public surprises ever. The plan was for Caron to bring all of us on stage with her and introduce her family to the world. We didn't know that the surprise was going to be on us. One that was rolled up inside a tragedy too horrible for any of us to ever truly get over. All of our lives were going to change forever.

Chapter Twenty

Backstage at Caron's concert in Milika all of us were extremely excited. Everyone in the family was there including Mama. "I can't believe," began Mya happily, "that I'm actually here at a Caron Cato concert. It just doesn't seem real." "You'll know it's real when you see her on stage," said Angel smiling. We were so happy that night. "I can't believe it myself," replied Dami. We didn't see Zane anywhere because Caron had gotten rid of him and Lumell.

"How is everybody doing?" Rosco asked us as he walked past us to speak to a group of Photographers. "We're doing just fine," we answered him. Then Baron came backstage where we were. He looked very happy, too, and had every reason to be. The song he wrote for Caron was steadily climbing the music charts. It was expected to reach number one in no time. As he talked with us he started looking around the room.

"What's wrong, Baron?" asked Venna curiously. "I was wondering where Corinne is," he replied puzzled. "She should've been here by now." "I talked to her on the telephone earlier today," I told him. "She said she would be here by seven thirty." The concert was supposed to start at nine o'clock and be over by eleven thirty. "It's almost eight o'clock now," said Baron a little concerned. In everyone's excitement we never noticed the time. Baron called to Rosco who walked over to where we were.

"Do you know what's keeping Corinne, Ros?" Baron asked Roscoe. "Isn't she in her dressing room?" he asked Baron. "I'll go look," Baron told him. "She could be in there but we still should've seen her come in." Baron left us to see if Caron was in her dressing room. He came back a few minutes later as we were all still talking. He had a grave look on his face.

"Corinne's not here," Baron told Rosco. "That's strange," said Rosco. "She's never late for a show, never. Somebody better call her at the hotel where she's staying." Baron hurriedly left us to telephone Caron. Minda walked into the room where we were. All of us greeted her happily but it was easy to see that she was upset about something.

"Are you alright, Minda honey?" Mama asked her. "You look like you're upset about something." "Oh," replied Minda, "I'm always like this before a concert. Just ask Rosco." Rosco confirmed what she said by nodding his head. However, a concerned look was still on his face. Other people connected with the show started getting nervous wondering where Caron was. "I-I'm sure she'll be here soon," Minda said. As we waited for Caron to come the clock was ticking. It was going on eight thirty when Baron returned to where we were. There was a worried look on his face.

"Did you talk to her?" Rosco asked him anxiously. "There was no answer in her hotel room," replied Baron. "Somebody better get over there," said Rosco, "to see what the problem is." "I'll go," volunteered Angel. "Yeah," I said, "I'll go with you." "Oh no," cried Mya out of the blue. "What?" I said as everyone looked at her. "Oh," she replied quickly, "it's nothing. You two better go." I noticed a strange look on Mya's face suddenly. She didn't say anything but I could tell that something was wrong. My friend knew something that nobody else did at the time. I will always admire her for knowing when to speak and when not to.

Angel and I took one of the limousines hired by the record company to the hotel where

Caron was staying. We went to the front desk and asked them to ring her room for us. When they did there was still no answer. "That's odd," replied the Manager. "It's been really busy here today but we still would have seen Miss Cato if she left the hotel."

"Can we get the key to her room?" asked Angel. "She's our sister." Both the Manager and the Clerks at the counter looked shocked and surprised when he said that. "Why sure," said the Manager smiling, "but I have to go with you. It's the hotel's policy you know." "Of course," replied Angel. As the three of us got into the elevator to go up to Caron's suite a heavy feeling came over me out of nowhere. It felt like all of the life went out of me suddenly. "You okay, Zo?" asked Angel as he looked at me. All I could do was slowly nod my head.

Caron's suite was on the ninth floor, room 903. The Manager opened the door to the suite and we entered. We called out to Caron but got no answer. It was eerily quiet. We went from one room to the other looking for her but we didn't see her. As I looked around what I thought was a wig on the floor caught my eye. It was protruding from an open closet in the bedroom. I walked closer to it in order to investigate. As I did I noticed that the "wig" was covered in what looked like blood. I stopped dead in my tracks.

"Y-you g-guys!" I yelled out nervously. Angel and the Manager came running into the room where I was. "What is it, Zo?" Angel asked looking at me. My brother and the Manager followed my stunned gaze. "Oh, my God," whispered the Manager horrified. "Oh, my God." I watched as he and Angel walked over to the closet and opened the door. There lay Caron on the floor of the closet. She was soaked in blood from her head down to her feet. What I thought was a wig was Caron's long dark hair. We realized she was dead.

I heard a terrifying and blood-curdling scream that was heard all over the ninth floor I was told later. It sounded far away to me. Angel told me that I was the one who screamed.

We always hoped and prayed that what Mya told us would never come to pass yet it did.

I went into shock immediately. At first I couldn't remember anything that happened that night. I was numb and in a stupor for many days. As gently as possible my family members and Mya told me all that happened. I really don't think it really sank in until Caron's funeral a week later.

It was a private service for Caron's family and closest friends. She made it clear in her Will that she wanted no big fanfare at her passing. Yet, the media made a tremendously big deal out of it. My siblings and I sat on the first rows of the church where Caron's body laid in state. Also, we met my Dad's other children.

Everything Caron had she left to me, Angel, Lee, Dami, Venna and Gina. Although she, Aziel and Zuroi knew about one another they never did have a chance to meet. There was no anger on the part of our other siblings because there was no mention of them in the Will. They hadn't spoken to Caron in years. We talked with all of them at the service, at the cemetery and at the repast. They liked us and we liked them. We promised to keep in touch with each other as well. I'm happy to say it was a promise that all of us would keep.

Mama came to the funeral with us for support. She spoke with our other siblings, too. We learned that all of their resentment because of what happened between our parents had been gone for years. Unforgiveness is such a tragic waste of time in people's lives especially when life is so short. Caron knew that, too, because she told me so.

Baron took Caron's death harder than anybody else did. I wondered what would have happened if he had been the one to find her body. After the funeral we didn't hear from him or anything about him for a long time. Rosco informed us that after the funeral Baron decided to leave the country for a while.

I noticed at the services for Caron that things seemed to be very strained between Angel and Minda. My brother kept eyeing her strangely for some reason. I couldn't understand what that was all about at first. Before they seemed to be close now it was as if they had drifted apart. Even before Caron's murder they hardly spoke to one another anymore. Minda didn't seem to care one way or the other and neither did Angel.

"Something is happening between those two," I started thinking about Angel and Minda. Nobody could have begun to guess what the problem was. I recalled the way Minda acted the last time she was at our house and how Mama questioned Angel about it. I was so lost in my thoughts I didn't hear Mya talking to me.

"Did you hear me, Zo?" asked Mya while we were at the cemetery. We watched as they lowered Caron's coffin into her grave. "No," I said looking at her through my tears. "What were you saying, Mya?" She had tears in her own eyes.

"Sometimes," she continued sadly, "I wish I couldn't see the things that I do. It can feel like a curse at times." I hugged her. "It's not your fault what you were born with, Mya," I replied gently. "In a way it is a blessing." "How's that?" she said confused. "You warned us that this was coming," I told her, "even if we didn't want it to. I believe in a way it softened the blow for us." Silently, I started to wonder if there was a reason forcefully so many violent deaths in a family. Our father was the common link between us. *"Maybe,"* I thought, *"there's a curse on our family because of what he did."* I quickly pushed the thought out of my mind. If there was such a thing I'm sure Mama wouldn't have escaped it. And no matter what he did my Dad was a good man with a good heart.

After everything was over with Caron we rarely saw Minda at all. However, we often overheard Angel arguing with someone on the telephone. It wasn't hard for us to know he was quarreling with a woman or who the woman was. It was like for some reason my

brother couldn't stand Minda anymore. We were wondering what she did to him. As far as

I knew the rest of us were still on good terms with her. Mama asked her to come over so

they could talk and she did.

I was at home with my mother on the day that Minda came over but Mama made

sure that Angel was not at home. When we saw Minda she looked terrible. She lost a

lot of weight, had dark circles under her eyes and was unusually jittery. A far cry from the

person we had known for many years. Mama didn't beat around the bush as the three of

us sat down in the kitchen at the table.

"I was wondering," began Mama, "if you'll tell us what's going on with you and

my son, Minda." Minda tried to smile but it wasn't sincere. "I think we've just grown

apart, Mama Moran," replied Minda sadly. "He acts like he hates you," I chimed in. "That's

not how you guys were. For a while we even thought you two were in love."

"Yes," added Mama looking into Minda's eyes, "especially when you came back

into his life." Minda's eyes welled with tears. "Are you okay, Minda?" asked my mother

concerned. "I can't talk with you all," said Minda looking from Mama to me. Then her

eyes became hardened suddenly. "None of you so please just let this alone. Please."

My mother covered Minda's hand with hers.

"You can talk to us, honey," Mama continued coaxing Minda to talk. "I wish things

were that easy," replied Minda almost angrily, "but they aren't. Eventually people find

out the truth. No matter how hard you try to hide it, right?" "What do you mean, hon?"

asked Mama. All Minda did was smile that forced smile at us as she stood up to leave.

"I still love all of you," Minda told me and my mother. "Nothing will ever change that. Angel is the one person I could never hide from if you know what I mean.

He always knew me better than I know myself. I thought it was a blessing to have

somebody like that to love me and I loved them. But do you know what?" "What,

sweetie?" asked Mama. "It turned out," answered Minda, "to be something that I

would regret." My mother and I looked at each other confused as Minda promptly

left our house.

"We can try and see if Angel will talk, Mama," I said to my mother. "No," replied Mama

thoughtfully. "I have a feeling we should take Minda's advice and let this alone."

"Why?" I wanted to know anxiously. "Just like she said," replied Mama, "no matter how

hard you try to hide the truth it always comes out. Nobody knows that better than we do.

Let's just sit back and see where all of this goes." So that is exactly what we did.

Chapter Twenty One

A full blown investigation was launched into Caron's brutal murder. Immediately it was surmised that she knew her killer and had voluntarily let them into her suite at the hotel. There was no sign of forced entry and no record that she had ordered any kind of room service. Therefore, it was concluded that her killer had already been inside the suite with her for a while.

Caron and her killer were together inside that suite for at least three hours before her murder. They had gone through nearly two bottles of wine and at least three joints. Caron told me herself that often she got high before one of her concerts. It relaxed her a lot.

Of course the first suspects were Zane and Lumell. Everyone knew they had more than enough reason to kill Caron. After all, she had recently fired both of them. They were quickly ruled out as suspects when their alibis checked out. They were halfway around the world, laid up in a motel room together at the time of Caron's murder.

Everyone in Caron's entourage and on her payroll were thoroughly questioned by the police. Yet, for a while a cold-blooded killer was right in front of us and we didn't even know it. It was unbelievable.

When we saw Caron's autopsy report I went into shock all over again. I wasn't the only one either. Her murderer was a monster. I couldn't believe something like that was loose in the world walking around with human beings.

Angel wasn't coping well with Caron's killing. He began seeing a doctor who prescribed anti-depressants for him. He was given tranquilizers to help him sleep and ease his anxiety attacks both day and night. He did have children to think about. After some months he started to show signs of healing. When Minda vanished my brother really began to heal. It was Mama who realized before anybody else did that Angel's problem was not only losing Caron but was also somehow connected to Minda.

Caron was stabbed ninety three times with a knife that had a jagged edge the detectives told us. It was a knife that had something like rows of shark's teeth on it. The wounds didn't kill her immediately and she had many defensive wounds on her body. In the end she bled to death. She had been gagged, bound and burned with lit cigarettes even before she was stabbed. The killer poured bleach down Caron's throat as if they were trying to destroy her beautiful voice. Once she was dead they tried to hide her body inside the closet which made no sense, and there was only one killer.

Nearly a year later the psychopathic monster who murdered my beloved sister still had not been captured. All of us who loved Caron grew angry. Yet, we understood that the police were doing all they could do to bring us closure. They didn't know we would never have that because we would never have Caron back. In the meantime things changed tremendously for me and my family.

Because of Caron we would never be poor again. We lived the kind of life we used to dream about. We shared our riches with all of our other siblings whom we grew to love and appreciate having in our lives. Mama began to love them, too, and they grew to love her as well.

We moved out of our old house and into a much nicer and bigger one in an exclusive part of Harly. All of us had nice new homes and cars. Mama even learned how to drive so she could use hers. My mother and I still shared a home together. I hadn't experienced anything strange in a long time. I forgot a lot of things I was told by the dead until I had a disturbing dream one night. At least I thought I was dreaming.

In the dream it was just breaking dawn. I got up and decided to go downstairs. Mama was sitting at the kitchen table sipping a cup of coffee like she usually did. "Good morning, Zo," she said looking up as I entered the room. "Good morning, Mama," I said smiling at her. "Would you like to see the newspaper this morning?" she asked me. "I guess so," I replied as I sat down at the table. "There's probably nothing new in it as usual. I don't know why they insist on calling it news." Mama chuckled softly.

The headline on the front page of the newspaper blared at me in big, bold, black letters, **'YEAR OLD MURDER OF CELEBRITY SOLVED'**. My mouth fell open in shock. I looked at Mama and said, "Did you see this, Mama?" She looked at the headline. "Oh yes," she said, "didn't I tell you? They caught Caron's killer." Someone walked into the kitchen behind where I was sitting. When I turned around Caron was standing there smiling at me. I was so happy to see her I got up and threw my arms around her hugging her tightly.

"Oh, Caron," I cried happily. "I miss you so much." I kissed her on her cheek. "I miss you, too, Zo," Caron said hugging me back. "I'm so glad you're here," I continued. "Sit down with us." Caron sat down with me and Mama at the table. We laughed and talked for what seemed like hours. I was ecstatic that she was there.

Finally Mama said, "Wow, look what time it is." I looked up at the clock on the wall and it was eleven thirty. "You'd better get dressed, Zo," continued Mama, "you and Caron might decide to go out for a while." "Yeah," replied Caron. "I'll have to leave you soon, Zo." "Alright," I said, "come on Caron. I'm not letting you out of my sight. You can help me get dressed." I took Caron by the hand as we got ready to leave the room.

"Don't forget to read the paper," my mother said to Caron and I as we were leaving the room. "Oh," I said, "that's right." I reached for the newspaper on the kitchen table and glanced at part of the story. "It's unreal," said Mama. "Who would've thought?" "That's right," replied Caron. "I certainly never thought she would've murdered me." In the newspaper story about Caron I saw part of the name of the person responsible for her murder. In disbelief it was the name *'Minda'* in bold, black letters. I woke up, opened my eyes and saw Mama walking into my room.

"Zo," said Mama, "are you alright now? You seemed like you were a little out of it earlier. What did you see in the newspaper that shook you up so much?" "What?" I said confused and groggy as I sat up in my bed. "Yeah," continued Mama, "I gave you half of a sleeping tablet to come you down. Then you came upstairs and went back to bed. I've been checking on you ever since then."

"You mean," I said, "I was really downstairs in the kitchen this morning with you, Mama?" "Zo," said Mama, "are you sure you're alright? Of course you were in the kitchen with me this morning. You saw something in the newspaper that upset you very much. What was it?" I didn't know what to say at first. "Caron was there, Mama," I blurted out softly. My mother grew pale as she sat down on the side of my bed.

"What did you see in the newspaper, honey?" Mama asked me concerned. "I looked at it but I didn't see whatever it was that you saw." "I thought I was dreaming,

Mama," I said, "but it was real. Caron was really here. I guess it's the only way she could tell somebody who killed her." "What did you see, honey?" she asked me again.

Tears began to well in my eyes as I looked at my mother. "Minda murdered Caron, Mama," I said to her softly. "That's what I saw in the newspaper. It was a story about Caron's murder and Minda was named as her killer." Mama put her hand to her chest in shock. "Oh, my God," she whispered in disbelief. "That must have been what was wrong between Angel and her. He suspected Minda from the beginning."

Caron's spirit came to me that morning in a way that I wouldn't be afraid. I thought it was a dream but it wasn't. Mama never saw or heard Caron or saw what I did in the newspaper. None of that really happened. Neither one of us could believe that Minda murdered Caron. Yet, all we had to do was remember everything Mya told us and the day when Minda started acting so strangely. The problem was how to prove it. Who would believe Caron had returned from the grave to help catch her murderer?

"What do we do now, Mama?" I asked my mother. "We can't just come out and accuse somebody but Caron wouldn't come back for nothing." "I know," replied Mama. "It's a shame she didn't tell you how to go about this. Maybe Angel can help us. I know he will. The way he feels about Minda." "Maybe," I said, "that's why he got so sick. He knew but could never prove it or do anything about it."

My mother set things in motion after that. She was more determined than anybody else to make Minda pay for what she did. First, we had to find out where she disappeared to.

Angel came up with the best idea and Mama and I agreed with him. "It seems that the best thing to do," he said, "is to enlist more of Caron's help." "How do we do that?" asked Mama. Both of them looked at me. Now was the time for courage and I knew just who to call on.

"Alright," I said. "I'll telephone Mya." When I told my friend what happened and what we needed to do she was eager to help us. In the end it was Caron who truly helped us. It was comforting to know that our loved ones who pass away are always around us especially when we need their comfort and help the most.

Chapter Twenty Two

The terrible knowledge about Minda held by Mama, Angel and I we told to

Mya. She was not the least bit shocked or surprised. "I knew all along," said Mya, "that

something was up with her. She started getting more and more jealous of the guys around

Caron. When Baron came on the scene she became psychotic where Caron was concerned.

It was all wrong the way she started acting. Caron had to go to Rosco a couple of

times about Minda's behavior toward her." We never knew anything about that and Rosco

never said anything. At some point Minda was out of control.

"What can we do to get this out there?" I asked Mya. "People have to know what

Minda did. Then Caron's murder will be solved and we can all move on." "I don't know,

honey," replied Mama, "short of Caron herself coming back to tell us what actually

happened in that hotel suite." "That is exactly what has to happen," replied Mya matter

of factly. "It's no use in us trying to play detective now since it's a year after the crime."

None of us wanted to acknowledge what we were all thinking. But other than that we

had no other options. "I think a séance is ridiculous," said Mama, "and I really don't

want to be a part of that." "I agree," replied Angel. I had to admit that I didn't want any

part of something like that either. It was un-Godly.

"Well," said Mya, "let's at least think about it before we make a final decision. It may

be our only chance. You know I'm willing to do it if it's what you all want." No one said anything. Then Mama broke the silence as she looked at Angel and I.

"Caron was your sister," began my mother softly, "and you loved her just like she loved you. I'll support any decision you make to resolve this problem. Lord Knows, that girl has already gotten away with this for too long." "Thanks, Mama," said Angel sadly. "Does anyone know where Minda is?" I asked. "Oh," said Mya, "she'll be coming back to Harly shortly. She thinks things have cooled down now and everybody has moved on with their lives. It won't be long." We didn't have to ask her how she knew that.

Mya was right on the money again. Two weeks later her, Mama, Angel and I were sitting in the kitchen when the telephone rang and Mama answered it. "Well, Minda," she said into the telephone receiver surprised, "it's been a long time." Since we were already forewarned by Mya none of us were really surprised to hear from Minda.

As it turned out we didn't need to do anything for more of Caron's help. Everything seemed to fall neatly into place for us from the day Mama got that phone call from Minda. It was as if someone other than us was controlling everything that lead up to Minda paying for her horrific crime.

"Why," said Mama into the telephone receiver, "sure you can come over, hon. I'll be glad to see you." My mother was eyeing all of us as she listened while Minda spoke to her on the other end of the phone line. I had to give it to Mama. She was great at acting as though nothing was wrong. "Well," said Mama, "I don't have anything to do with what goes on between you and Angel. But you're welcome to visit. You know that."

Mama slowly shook her head at us as she continued to listen to Minda on the phone again. "Yes," she spoke, "I'll be here this Friday evening. Some of the family might be here, too." They finished their telephone conversation and Mama hung up the phone. As she sat back down at the kitchen table she tried not to show her anger.

"You mean to tell me," began Angel angrily looking at my mother, "she has the audacity to want to come to see us again?" There was absolute disdain for Minda in my brother's voice. Things had changed so much between them it was unbelievable.

"This Friday night," replied Mama shaking her head again. "That's when she'll finally pay," said Mya smiling a crooked smile at us. "What?" I asked her a little confused. "How?" "I can tell you this," replied Mya looking at the rest of us. "We don't need a séance. In fact, we won't need to do anything because Caron *is* going to help us." She didn't elaborate but we got the impression that Caron's spirit was there with us.

It was a little scary. I became nervous and anxious as the night of Minda's upcoming visit approached. I could hardly wait. I didn't know what was going to happen to bring Minda to justice for Caron's murder. But everyone knew that Mya was never wrong about anything she told us. We wanted Minda, in the worst way, to know the pain that she caused when she took Caron from our lives. Her blatant boldness was unreal. She killed our sister, hid away and now wanted to smile and grin in our faces.

I found it mind-boggling when I recalled how Minda came to Caron's funeral services. She sat through the entire event as well as the repast right along with us. Suddenly we realized that Minda didn't know Caron was our sister. Angel never told her nor did any of the rest of us. No one really knew but us, not even the media. Because she was murdered Caron never got the chance to publicly reveal and confirm that information to the world like she wanted to. *"I can't wait,"* I thought smiling to myself,

"to tell Minda about Caron and us."

Chapter Twenty Three

We were not sure what was going to happen that night. Mama told no one else about my vision or about Minda. In fact, my mother made sure we would have no other visitors by telling our family and friends that she and I were going out that night. Mama didn't usually outright lie but this was too important to leave anything to chance. It was all we could do to stop watching the clock on the wall as we sat quietly in the living room waiting. My excitement had to be showing but Mama, Angel and Mya were as cool as cucumbers. It was so quiet in the room.

Suddenly a soft, gentle hand brushed across my cheek and startled me. No one was sitting near me so I realized Caron's spirit was in the room with us. I smiled. When I looked at Mya she was smiling at me. "Yes," she said to me, "it's her, Zo." I felt tears well in my eyes. "She's really here?" Angel asked looking at Mya anxiously. Mya nodded her head. "Where?" he wanted to know. My mother smiled at us. "She's sitting next to Zo," Mya told my brother. He looked toward me.

"Hey, Caron," Angel said softly to Caron's spirit as he choked back his tears. The room became unusually warm to the point where we began to sweat. Suddenly where Angel was sitting we saw an impression in the cushion next to him. We knew Caron was sitting next to him. The whole room filled up with a loving feeling that none of us would ever be able to describe. My brother tried to wipe his tears away but they wouldn't stop. The doorbell rang and jolted us back to what we were supposed to be doing. Mama went to answer the door.

At first I thought Angel was going to blow our whole plan but he managed to quickly pull himself together. None of us truly realized he'd begun to hate Minda. Yet, he didn't let us down because he knew how important it was for us to get Minda Banger. Mama entered the room again with Minda following her. Needless to say, she panicked when she saw Mya but quickly tried to hide it. We greeted her as we usually did. Immediately Minda shivered.

It was strange since the rest of us were sweating because of the warmth in the room from Caron's presence. "Are you okay, hon?" Mama asked her. "It's chilly in here to me," said Minda, "but I see that you're all sweating." "Is that right?" said Angel sarcastically as he glared at Minda. "No," replied Mama, "the temperature in here is just fine." Before Mama sat down and without Minda suspecting anything she made sure the tape recorder we hid earlier was turned on.

Our conversation started out normally as it always had with Minda. "I-I didn't know you would be here, Mya," said Minda nervously looking at Mya. "Oh well," replied Mya with a forced smile, "you know me and Zo are practically inseparable." We were looking for a way to approach Minda with the subject of Caron's murder. I should have known Mya could always be counted on.

"It seems like we should all have something to drink," said Mya. "That's a good idea," replied Mama as if on cue. "Why don't we have some iced tea?" She went into the kitchen and came back with a tray of glasses and a pitcher of iced tea. Then she poured a glass of it for each one of us and gave it to us. As we started to sip it Minda's glass was forcefully knocked right out of her hand to the floor. She was terrified as she jumped up from her chair and looked at the rest of us. It was easy for her to surmise that none of us had done it. The horror on her face was priceless.

"Yeah," said Angel standing up and glaring angrily into Minda's eyes, "the one you killed did that, Minda. Caron is right here with us. You never knew she was our sister." Minda's eyes were filled with absolute terror. She tried to leave the room but my brother stood in front of her daring her to move.

"Don't you even think about trying to get away again," Angel said to Minda through clenched teeth. She looked around the room wide-eyed and scared. I guessed it was the way Caron looked when she realized Minda was going to kill her and there was no way for her to get help. After that she slumped down into the chair and started to sob hysterically. We saw the guilt that she had been carrying. Sometimes criminals really do *want* to get caught. They're so tired of trying to run away from what they've done.

"Why, Minda?" Mama asked her gently but angry, too. "Why did you murder Caron? Why?" Minda stopped sobbing and looked at us. She was truly pathetic. "Your sister?" she said in disbelief. "Caron was really your sister? One of your Dad's other kids?" Minda always knew our father had other children besides us so that was nothing new. A sad, crooked smile came across her lips that were trembling as she stared into space. It looked as if she was seeing something that the rest of us couldn't see and I guessed that she was. She began to speak.

"I was in love with Caron for a long time," began Minda softly still staring into space. It was like she was in a daze. "All I wanted was for her to love me back. She told me that she did love me but not like I wanted her to. Women were not her thing she said. I thought once Zane was out of the picture she would change, and maybe give me a shot but in walked Baron Bonds. She said he was the love of her life. I told her

that he could never have any children. He was sterile and never believed any woman

would want him. She was surprised to find that out but said she didn't care. I was the only

one he ever told about that but I thought she should know. So I spent almost the whole afternoon with

her before her show that night. I just wanted to be alone with her at least for a while. I thought

I could change her mind about me."

"So," said Angel angrily, "Caron told you to get lost and you decided to kill her? Is

that your reason for what you did to her, Min? Are you serious? I should kill *you*!" Mama

hurriedly got up and wrapped her arms around my brother to calm him down. If she hadn't

I believe to this day that my brother would have killed Minda right there on the spot. It didn't

make sense for him to go to jail, too.

"All I wanted was for her to love me back like I loved her," continued Minda softly

as if she hadn't heard Angel. It was then that we knew she was unstable. "I waited for her

for a very long time hoping she would just look my way. I never felt that way about anybody before

you know. I had to do it. I couldn't let anybody else have her." After saying that she buried

her face in her hands and started sobbing softly. It was a pitiful sight.

"How dare you, you lousy bitch!" cried Angel with great rage and bitterness. "How dare

you murder our sister for some stupid, pathetic, idiotic reason like that!" My brother

started for Minda in a rage. "Angel, no!" cried Mama holding him back. "She's a sick girl,

sweetie. We'll just call the police. Okay?" Angel broke down as he slumped into a chair.

Mama gently rubbed his back as angry, bitter tears ran down his face. All of us began crying

as I called the detectives who were working Caron's case. It was such a senseless, terrible

tragedy that occurred and one that none of us deserved especially Caron. She had finally found some peace and joy in her life when it was needlessly snuffed out.

When I came back into the room the warmth in there had increased. We knew Caron's spirit was still there with us as we heard the police sirens approaching our house. As they came into the house and handcuffed Minda my mother gave them the recording of her confession. Our hope was that she wouldn't get off on an insanity plea like what happened with my Dad, Devon and Patsie.

Minda was an emotionally and mentally disturbed young woman and had been that way for a long time. It was amazing that none of us ever saw it. And, it was unfortunate that Caron became the target of a crazed delusion that she had about her. Angel confided in us some time later that he suspected many times that Minda might have had mental issues. Yet, he had no idea how severe they were. When his suspicions were realized it was too late.

"I should've tried to get her some kind of help," said Angel calming down as we watched the cops take Minda away in the police car. "It's not your fault," replied Mya compassionately. "You can't blame yourself anymore than I can. If anyone should've seen it, it should've been me. I always felt something was off about her but I could never put my finger on it." Angel smiled at her. After that night he never needed pills or doctors anymore. Justice for Caron was what truly and totally healed my brother.

The flashing lights from the police vehicles attracted attention to our home. Also, our other family members rushed to our house wondering what had happened. As all of us sat around the living room, which we now called the *'sitting room'*, Mama and I told them about everything that had occurred. I don't have to tell you how numb with shock and disbelief all of them were.

Six months later Minda Banger went on trial for the first degree murder of

Corinne Atocano a.k.a Caron Cato. My family and I sat in that courtroom every day of her trial

listening to every horrid detail of Caron's brutal murder. It wasn't easy to do but we did it. Minda

looked as if she was somewhere else instead of there on trial for murder. Even when she

was sentenced to die in the gas chamber for what she did to Caron she remained emotionless.

She was a tortured soul forced to live in a world where she didn't want to be. It was so sad.

When the judge asked her if she wanted to say something to Caron's family Minda

just shook her head 'no'. That's the last we ever saw or heard of her.

On the day after the trial was over I went to the cemetery. Caron loved carnations so I

placed a bunch of them on top of her grave. The headstone had a big musical note carved

into it. It read: *Corinne Mavis Atocano, Beloved Sister and Friend* and of course

her birth date and date of death. "I love you, Caron Cato," I whispered. "I wish we'd

had more time together." I shuddered as I felt a presence there so I looked up.

There was Caron standing there smiling at me. "Me, too, Zo," she said. "Me, too." As I

looked over her shoulder I saw my Dad, Devon, Patsie and Bedelia. All of them were

smiling as they waited for Caron to join them. Just as suddenly as they

appeared they were gone. I have never seen or heard from any of them since that day

and neither has Mya. I know now that as long as everything is alright

with the people they love and have left behind the dead are at peace, and that's a great thing.

THE END

www.ingramcontent.com/pod-product-compliance
Lightning Source LLC
Chambersburg PA
CBHW020116310726
48970CB00002B/667